Nancy & Nick

CAROLINE B. COONEY

SCHOLASTIC BOOK SERVICES
New York Toronto London Auckland Sydney Tokyo

Cover Photo by Owen Brown

ISBN 0-590-31981-7

12 11 10 9 8 7 6 5 4 3 2 1 1 2 3 4 5 6/8

Printed in the U.S.A. 06

Nancy & Nick

A Wildfire Book

WILDFIRE TITLES
FROM SCHOLASTIC

Love Comes to Anne by Lucille S. Warner
I'm Christy by Maud Johnson
That's My Girl by Jill Ross Klevin
Beautiful Girl by Elisabeth Ogilvie
Superflirt by Helen Cavanagh
A Funny Girl Like Me by Jan O'Donnell
Just Sixteen by Terry Morris
Suzy Who? by Winifred Madison
Dreams Can Come True by Jane Claypool Miner
I've Got a Crush on You by Carol Stanley
An April Love Story by Caroline B. Cooney
Dance with Me by Winifred Madison
One Day You'll Go by Sheila Schwartz
Yours Truly, Love, Janie by Ann Reit
The Summer of the Sky-Blue Bikini by Jill Ross Klevin
I Want to Be Me by Dorothy Bastien
The Best of Friends by Jill Ross Klevin
The Voices of Julie by Joan Oppenheimer
Second Best by Helen Cavanagh
A Kiss for Tomorrow by Maud Johnson
A Place for Me by Helen Cavanagh
Sixteen Can Be Sweet by Maud Johnson
Take Care of My Girl by Carol Stanley
Lisa by Arlene Hale
Secret Love by Barbara Steiner
Nancy & Nick by Caroline B. Cooney

One

My mother collects kitchen antiques. An investment, she says. Personally, I think an investment is something you'd be willing to sell, but nothing would induce Mother to part with any of her collection.

Last week we took one of our usual fourteen-hour Saturday excursions to the mountains, supposedly (as always) to admire the laurels and rhododendrons, but really to scour the Blue Ridge for any antique shops that might have popped up since our last trip there. Mother found a very early Jell-O box and a wire carpet beater with an entirely different shape from any of her other carpet beaters. She also spotted a very old Moravian cookie cutter shaped like a hand, but by then we were broke.

Also, I was reminding her at five-minute intervals that the remaining cash had to buy me a new pair of shoes, because my toes were becoming slowly deformed in my old pair. You could see that Mother was really torn between having a daughter with bent toes and owning that cookie cutter. I will be the only girl in town whose mother thinks of cookie cutters every time she looks at my feet.

When we get back home from our typical excursions we stagger into the apartment, trembling with driving fatigue. But this week, thank goodness, we went to Richmond, which is only an hour away. Sensible people go there quite often. Of course, sensible people are going to art museums or concerts or visiting civilized friends, while we are hitting the flea markets.

I am not a connoisseur of flea markets (connoisseurs presumably like the thing they're expert in) but I have been to my share of them. I think it would be fair to say I have been to about one hundred times my share of them. They're all alike. Booth after booth of garbage — old tacky junky stuff from a box somebody's aunt meant to throw out in 1964 but forgot and stashed in a corner and now they want two years' worth of your allowance for every scrap of it. When my mother sees a booth like that, her eyes kind of glaze over and her breath comes faster. She is totally transported with the belief that somewhere in that heap of junk is a genuine find.

She paws, strokes, taps, and fingers every object she sees. And at a flea market, that's a lot of objects. I come along not to buy and not to browse, but to keep Mother from spending the rent money.

"Nancy! Psssst!" Mother was giving me her

frantic but coolly disguised as totally bored look. This meant she had found a find.

"Yes, Mother?" I strolled over. I am well-trained. We each picked up a piece of Depression glass and fondled it while Mother whispered in my ear. "Those books, Nancy — silly woman has those books marked for only two dollars apiece."

Now if it were a Rolls Royce Silver Cloud, I might be able to tell if it was underpriced. These books, however, were tired-looking Book-of-the-Month-Club editions of ten-year-old best sellers. "That's why there are libraries, Mother," I said. "So you can read that stuff free."

"No, no, no, *no,* Nancy." She was quite put out with me. Setting down the Depression glass, she lost all caution and led me to the book row. From between *The Robe* and *What's New in Color Photography: 1963,* she drew out a slim worn volume that had once been pale blue with tiny flowers in a diagonal latticework. About a third of the way down the front of the cover was a large light rectangle with lacy corners. It contained the title in tangled complex script: *The Nearing River Chapter of the Daughters of the Confederacy Cookbook of 1915.*

"Whee," I said dutifully.

Mother, obviously wafted to kitchen antiques heaven, smiled dreamily.

When the century was young, women's clubs and church groups loved to put together cookbooks. A fair number of these have survived and Mother feels it is her purpose here on earth to perpetuate the survival rate. We have, I believe, eighty-three ancient cookbooks. Mother reads them over and over, lovingly, the way other women read romances and gothics. Mother loves the recipes, the advertisements, the contributors' names, the peculiar measurements, the illustrations, the little family histories that can sometimes be deduced from odd paragraphs here and there . . . but she detests actually cooking. *That,* at least, is a feeling with which I can identify.

While I maneuvered through the late-afternoon traffic, Mother sat in the passenger seat happily muttering to herself about Miss Mary H. Metcalf's receipt for Boiled Cider Pie. It's sort of like driving with the radio on. After a while you don't notice it.

I am always the driver in our little duo. Mother hates to drive. She wants *me* to drive so *she* can look out the window and spot little hand-painted antique shop signs. It would be nice if she would spot them before I am past the turn, but she never does.

Mother thought the nicest thing in my life was my sixteenth birthday and the acquisition of a license. Everybody else's parents were postponing the evil day, moaning about Freedom, the Misuse of; or Gas, the High Cost of; or Cars, the Privilege and Responsibility of. But my mother had me at the Motor Vehicle Bureau at dawn on my birthday, fee in hand. By noon of the day I got my temporary license, we had already parallel-parked in front of three antique shops with Mother joyously and—as it turned out—permanently ensconced in the passenger seat.

"Nancy, guess what?"

"Mother, wait till I'm out of this traffic circle, okay?"

"Nancy, just listen to this."

"Mother, that furniture van is going to eat our bumper. Wait a minute." I sometimes think that having children will come as no shock to me. I have always driven a car with an immature person babbling at me.

"Nancy, the woman who donated the recipe for cough syrup is named Nearing. Miss Elizabeth Priory Nearing."

I avoided the furniture van, extricated myself from the traffic circle, honked at a dachshund deliberating whether to cross the street, and accelerated quickly to avoid a crash with a guy in an old Triumph who was jumping the light. "How *about* that?" I said.

But Mother went on, "I wonder . . . I wonder if we're related."

I hadn't even paid attention to the name of that particular recipe donor. *Our* last name is Nearing. Father died years ago. Mother had never met any of his family and we'd never come across anybody else named Nearing. I said, "If she donated a recipe to a cookbook that was published in 1915, I very much doubt she is still with us."

"She may have had descendents."

"In 1915, Mother, people named Miss did not have descendents."

"She could have been young in 1915. She could have gotten married later and had children."

I've always envied people with families. You

just know that at Thanksgiving they're gathered around the dining room table, kissing their fourth cousins, embracing their aunts, and generally reveling in all those roots. If you had a big family there'd always be somebody to babysit for or to do your babysitting. There'd always be little kids' stockings to make neat little presents for and somebody who could teach you to knit or take you to New York or organize a family soccer team or tell you the name of a good automobile mechanic they trust.

Mother and I have each other.

Fortunately I like Mother. It's always good to like the person with whom you share a four-room apartment that is hung, strewn, and jammed with little antiques. I have a bolt on the inside of my bedroom door so the antiques can't slither in during the night. Grow them on your side of the apartment, I tell Mother.

Mother tells me I should have a hobby myself, Everyone needs a hobby, she insists; hobbies make a person well-rounded.

My hobby, I tell her, is daydreaming about boys. Someday I plan to expand this hobby to include a real live boy. But this seems to require the consent of the boy, and so far this hasn't happened.

My favorite study hall activity is thinking of interesting names for a boy to have. Then I see how Nancy Nearing would look linked with it. Oh Nancy, says my mother sadly, when she finds my little lists. Take up classical music or transmission repair. Something you can really benefit from.

I tell her I would truly benefit from having a boyfriend.

I drove the last several miles home from Richmond daydreaming that Miss Elizabeth Priory Nearing had married late in life and had a son. He came down with a terrible lung disease, but she saved him with her famous cough remedy. He grew up and also had a son and we would meet and the family would be complete once more. I almost went through a red light trying to work out how many generations I was going to need for this fantasy to work right.

"We're home, Mother." I slid the little car between the custom van with triangle windows that belongs to the two young men in the apartment above us and the gas-guzzling chrome-studded ship that belongs to the retired couple in the apartment below us.

"Nancy, you *must* read this cookbook," said my mother, as if cookbook reading were on a par with good citizenship and voting.

"Sure," I said. I locked the car. We ran up the stairs, something Mother often does fifteen times in a row. Exercise, she explains when people begin to regard her nervously. Keeps the old heart pumping. Or stops it, she gets told. Anyway, we ran up.

"Really, Nan," she said again, "I want you to read this cookbook."

"Mother, I have a term paper due on Lord Byron." Cookbook reading is very very low on my list of things to read even when I'm not doing a paper on Lord Byron. Besides, cooking is too detestable even to think about. One of my life goals is to be rich enough to eat all my meals out.

"But, Nannie," Mother said (and I knew she really wanted it, the way she was going through all my nicknames), "Nannie, this book is about you, you'll love it."

It was difficult to imagine how a cookbook compiled in 1915 could be about me. I shooed Mother out of my room and began concentrating on Lord Byron. I don't know why English teachers think Byron is so interesting. Every single poem of his I've ever read is a complete dud. I wondered what the teacher would say if I handed him a paper that began, "For reasons not made clear in research texts, this conceited fellow — possibly through the aid of a good press agent — got his poems published."

I probably would not get an A.

After I had written the word *dud* in fat curving letters and added little birds and flowers and leaves, like a medieval manuscript, I decided that maybe a cookbook about me would be more interesting than Lord Byron. I opened my bedroom door. "Mother," I said (you never have to yell in an apartment as small as ours), "what makes you say that cookbook is about me?"

She was right there, putting the cookbook in my hand.

My desk chair is on casters. I love to propel myself around the bedroom. I set the cookbook on my lap and scooted back to my desk and shoved Lord Byron to the rear, where he belonged.

I began with the introduction. I don't normally read introductions — they're sure to be stuffy — but the word *Nearing,* my own last name, kept popping out at me.

It seemed that Nearing River was a town in North Carolina. The name had nothing to do with proximity to a body of water, although there was a river there. The town was founded by the Nearing family. Half the members of the Daughters of the Confederacy Chapter that compiled the cookbook seemed to be married to Nearings or sprung from Nearings or both. There was actually a biscuit recipe written by Anne Nearing Nearing.

I suddenly began thinking of the distant cousins and grandmothers with white hair and aprons and old cookie recipes that I'd daydreamed about during the drive home. (Though, in fact, all my friends' grandmothers are young with dark hair and buy their cookies at the grocery.)

And then came the real surprise.

The very first recipe had been put in by a Nearing lady who said she had gotten it from her grandmother: Nelle Catherine Nearing.

I was so startled I nearly tore the page in half and ruined Mother's investment.

Nelle Catherine Nearing is *my* name. Mother had wanted to call her new baby daughter Melissa, but Father, the father I can't remember, had insisted on Nelle Catherine. And after all that arguing to settle on such an old-fashioned name, he called me nothing but Nancy.

It was weird to find my own name scattered throughout a cookbook dated 1915. As far as I could piece it together, there were no fewer than four donors whose names were Nelle Catherine. I read every recipe in the little volume. Susannah Nearing had a sweet potato pie recipe. Nelle Catherine Nearing Roberson submitted a recipe using cold potatoes, something apparently unheard of, because she had to explain that she really did mean cold potatoes; she called her novelty potato salad. Elizabeth Mollison and Jeannie Nearing Brown had cake recipes and Constance Nearing Fitzhugh gave out hints on how to use the new electric irons that were just coming out. Kate Firth was cooking with gas now, which was her bread-making secret, and Nancy Nearing MacDonald told how to dry spices in the attic.

Nancy Nearing MacDonald had something else to say, too.

Since 1748, when the Nearings first came to North Carolina, the women had been named Nelle Catherine and nicknamed N.C., for their initials. "Nancy" was not a name at all, but a quick way of saying "N.C."

"Mother?" I said. I was actually breathing quickly and my hands were getting prickly. "Mother, do you really think this is me?"

"Nannie, how could it be anyone else? Your father insisted on naming you Nelle Catherine. But he would never call you anything but Nancy."

"But, Mother, if we are related to these Nearings, we must have rafts of relatives. Didn't Father ever say anything to you about them?"

"The only thing your father ever said to me about his past was that he had grown up in a small town and hated it. He never wanted to see another one again and wanted to make sure no wife or daughter of his was ever going to have to endure small town life."

"Mother, you've failed. We are unquestionably living in a small town."

"I think by comparison with wherever he came from, this is quite a city, Nan. I think small town means, you know, say, a thousand people. Or even less."

"We have twice that many people in our high school."

"Precisely. I wonder where Nearing River, North Carolina, is and how many people it has."

We grabbed the atlas and flipped to North Carolina. We pored through the town listings till we found Nearing River. F-7 on the grids. We ran our fingers over the page and there was a teeny tiny open circle with a teeny tiny label that said NEARING RIVER.

Mother got out her mileage pen and ran it down the thready little secondary roads leading from our home to Nearing River. "Not bad. Only a hundred and seventy miles. We'll go next Saturday."

"Mother," I said irritably, "one hundred seventy miles is not *only*. One hundred seventy miles is a *lot*."

"A town that produced a cookbook like that," murmured Mother. "It must be a nice place."

I began to get embarrassed just thinking about going there. What would Mother do? Cruise up and down the streets calling "Yoo-hoo, Nearings, here we are"? A woman who would run up and down the same stairs fifteen times in a row would do anything. I could just see us going into the banks and the post office demanding to meet all Nearings, especially those with the initials N.C.

"I wonder if Kate Firth's gas stove is still around," said Mother dreamily.

"Mother! We do not have room for an old stove in here!"

"Or Nancy Nearing MacDonald's spice jars." Her eyes took on a rhapsodic gleam. I have such a one-track mind. All I could wonder about was whether Nancy Nearing MacDonald had a handsome grandson. Or would he be a great-grandson?

Two

It may have been "only" one hundred seventy miles, but let me tell you, they were one hundred seventy hard, long, tough miles. "Mother, can't you ever take a turn driving?" I said desperately.

"Nancy, love, I'm trying to read that sign. Does it say hamburgers or antiques?"

"If it says hamburgers I'll stop."

"Antiques, Nan, antiques! Stop, stop!"

I refused to stop. My fingers had been wrapped around the steering wheel for three hours, and except for food I wasn't going to unwrap them until we tottered into Nearing River. Mother sat and sulked. I did battle with some wild teenagers in a dune buggy and an old lady in a Dodge Dart. After that I played footsie with a truck that was having a love affair with the dotted line in the middle of the road. When we finally hauled into Nearing River I had to sit and pant for a minute. Mother vaulted out right away, of course, and began scouring the village for antique shops.

When I had calmed down, I caught up to her. "For this I drove three and three-quarter hours?" I said, looking at the pitiful rundown main street that seemed to be all of Nearing River. Half the stores were unoccupied. The other half looked in dire need of customers. Probably it was like so many other downtown shopping areas: a shopping mall or two had ruined it.

"You should have made better time than that," said Mother. "Why do you drive so slowly, anyway?"

There seemed no point in mentioning the antagonists I'd encountered on the road. I concentrated on trying to find the river, creek, stream, or even swamp for which Nearing River could have been named, but there was no evidence of one.

"Ah ha!" said Mother triumphantly.

I need hardly say this is the exclamation that prefaces entrance into yet another antique shop. I tried to look interested in case any handsome young man were in there, although it is my experience (and let me tell you, I am experienced with antique shops) that it is a rare teenage boy who hangs out at an antique shop.

As a matter of fact, we didn't find *anybody* in the antique shop. It didn't take too long to putter through on our own. It wasn't Mother's kind of shop at all, featuring chairs for eight hundred dollars and candlestands for five hundred. I went back out on the sidewalk to look for hamburger signs, since starvation was rapidly setting in and candlestands do nothing for me even at ten dollars. I knew Mother would be at least another fifteen minutes. The true hunter does not give up easily. The harder it is to find a find, the harder the true antique hunter hunts. No doubt Mother was poking into every spider-webbed corner, opening drawers that hadn't worked in four generations.

She came out very dispiritedly. I handed her a damp washcloth. I always keep one in a plastic sandwich bag in my purse because she gets dusty hands, and if she has found something, without fail I am wearing a white shirt and she will be seized with the desire to hug me.

"No, huh?" I said. I was thinking how nice it was that there was nothing in Nearing River to buy. The place had something going for it after all. With all the money we had not spent on antiques, we could have an extra big lunch. And possibly a long and tasty afternoon snack. I don't know why Mother accuses me of having my mind on boys all the time. I think of food a lot, too.

"Ah ha!" said my mother.

"Oh, no," I groaned.

"Look at this, Nan!"

"I'm afraid to. What does it cost? Do we already have six of it?"

"Really, Nancy. You are so difficult. I can't remember why I always bring you along on these trips."

"You bring me along to drive."

"Oh. That's right. Well, anyway, look at that notice."

I cringed. If it was an auction, we were sunk. I would have to pick Mother's pocketbook if I wanted to have lunch the following week.

The notice was a faded old rectangle of poster-board with a photograph of something indistinguishable but square. It read, "The Historical Society of Nearing River is sponsoring a tour of the Nearing River House."

"What do they want for that piece of paper?" I said. "A hundred dollars?"

"Ding-a-ling. The paper isn't for sale."

"One of a kind, huh? Worth millions."

"Nancy," she said irritably, "you know perfectly well that notice is not an antique. It's a recent advertisement of an open house."

"Could have fooled me."

"The paper is sunbaked, that's all. Come on, let's go. According to the map there, it's just down the road and to the right and then to the left and you circle a little bit and it's on the right."

"What is?"

"The Nearing River House. Come on. We might miss the tour."

"*Mother!* That tour was obviously years ago. The owners of this shop are so sloppy they never got around to removing the notice."

"It says Saturdays. See? 'Tours on Saturdays.' "

I moaned from lack of nourishment.

"And even if they aren't giving tours the house is still there and we can poke around," she said, bounding into the car.

I detest touring historical houses. How many rope beds and bullet-riddled walls can a person admire? The tour guides are either plump old ladies, who tell you six hundred more things about the original owner of the house than you ever wanted to know, or else bored skinny Junior League volunteers, who can't tell you anything. Besides, you can't touch and Mother does anyway. Somebody is always scolding her and it embarrasses me so much I have to leave the tour and pretend what I like best is gardens.

"Let's have lunch," I said. "My stomach will growl through the whole tour."

"It's only eleven-thirty. Come on. We'll eat later."

My friends argue quite successfully with their parents. Holly is especially good at it. Her father says: No, Never, Certainly Not! And fifteen minutes later Holly is back on the phone saying: It's fine with them, Nan. Me, I always end up sighing and agreeing.

I studied the little map, verified the left and right turns and drove my mother to the historical house. Maybe I'd get lucky and they'd have a concession. Or at least a vending machine.

We went down a long drive bordered by the kind of fence that is stacked at angles and always looks as if it's falling down, even when the maintenance staff just fixed it yesterday. There was Nearing River House: your typical eighteenth-century Southern farmhouse. If you've toured one, you've toured them all. One room deep and two rooms wide, the lower floor divided by a wide porch–hall combination. Two bedrooms upstairs: one for parents and their current infant, the other for older children and for spinning and weaving. Outdoors: the kitchen, smokehouse, barn, and so forth. "You go in," I said to Mother, noting without interest that tours hadn't ended years ago after all and were in fact starting up again that moment. "I'll just sit here and admire the lilies."

"Irises," she said. "Try to be observant."

"Whatever."

"Nancy, I cannot abide it when you display such a bad attitude. Now get up this minute and come with me. It's open. I can see the tour guide on the porch. Nice long hair she has, too — see it shine in the sun? We'll ask her if she knows any Nearings."

"I'll go with you on the tour if you promise *not* to ask if she knows any Nearings."

"But, Nancy, that's why we drove down here. To find the other N.C. Nearings."

"Mother, I'll be too embarrassed. Don't ask anybody anything, promise?"

"Certainly not. I'll ask what I please. Now march."

Other people whose mothers address them like kindergartners would rightly refuse to cooperate. Mother looks and sounds daydreamy, but she definitely falls into your stereotyped Southern picture of the iron hand under the velvet glove. I seem to be velvet through and through.

Someday, I told myself, trailing after Mother past the irises and up onto the narrow porch, I am going to stand up to Mother. She is not right all the time. Sometimes I am right.

I walked up the steps, and there in the doorway the girl tour guide with the nice shiny long hair turned out to be a boy tour guide with nice shiny long hair.

Thank goodness I hadn't chosen this particular occasion to start my rebellion. The guide was the best-looking boy I had ever seen. He wore a loose white muslin shirt, dark baggy pants (breeches, I guess), old scuffed boots, and a cotton scarf at his neck. And his long, thick, honey-colored hair was tied in a Revolutionary War type ponytail with a leather thong.

And immediately I was embarrassed.

Whenever I see a good-looking boy I am impressed first and embarrassed second. I am never quite sure what embarrasses me, but I start blushing as if I had written down a dozen wild fantasies about him in a diary and he had just read it.

I couldn't even look at Mother to see what her reaction was to the long hair that belonged to a male. I couldn't take my eyes off the boy. He was my age, or a little older, and he was perfect.

For a moment I daydreamed that when he looked at me he would forget his speech about the Nearing River House, fall immediately in love with me, and stagger toward me. We would shock the bridge club (also touring the house) by going off together behind the English box shrub nestled beside the porch.

The boy had clearly given enough tours to be able to lead them in his sleep. "This," he said, "is called a dogtrot. It is the central hall and also a sleeping porch, with doors open at both ends, so that in the hot humid summers every possible breeze would be captured." He had the kind of trained voice that sounds so much like a tape you wonder why they don't just *use* a tape, and let you poke a button in each room. "The dog-trot also had safety uses, separating the fireplaces in the hope that if the house ever did catch fire it would be easier to put out." But in his case I could understand why they didn't use a tape. If you were bored by the fine fanlight over the front door, you could feast your eyes on the tour guide.

I feasted my eyes.

When he finally did look my way he didn't react in the slightest. He didn't cry out, ask me for a date, or even drop a syllable of his talk. I was so embarrassed about pretending he would that I blushed anyway. "Originally," he said, "the house faced east." His voice droned along. I wondered if other tours, other groups, were less boring to him. If sometimes a girl appeared on the tour who could put a spark in his boxed voice. "Therefore the door you came in was the back door when it was built and the finer molding and elaborate interior detail is on what is now the rear."

He was also tall, muscular, and had started — or ought to start — shaving. All I could think of was that his cheek was probably raspy-feeling. I had this terrible fear that when I moved past him into the parlor, I would actually touch his cheek to see if it was. "Notice the large double-shouldered Flemish bond chimneys," he said.

"Cute, huh?" my mother whispered.

"The chimneys?" I whispered back.

"Nancy, you are truly peculiar. The *boy*."

"Oh yes. Yes, he's okay." It's odd. Usually when Mother and I agree on something we admit it right away and grin. Now I couldn't bring myself to admit how terrific I thought this boy was. It was like Mother hunting for a find — when you do find it you don't admit it, in case the seller realizes you want it and charges you more.

I was actually standing there feeling nervous. As if saying how neat he was would jinx something. And the funny thing is, I hate it when a girl judges a boy just on his looks. If it were Holly falling in love at first sight I'd really be on her about it. I'd lecture her on personality and conversation and depth and manners and habits and how you couldn't possibly fall in love with somebody when all you've done is look at him and the only words he's uttered are out of a history text privately printed by a local historian.

I thought, he's perfect. I wonder what his name is.

"The wing chair by the fireplace," he said, "is a most interesting example of — "

I didn't think it was particularly interesting. Surely there were ten hundred more interesting things for someone like that to consider than wing chairs by the fireplace. Me, for example.

I wondered why he was leading tours of the Nearing River House. Perhaps his mother was president of the Historical Society and blackmailed him into it. Perhaps he was paid immensely well and was saving up to go to college. Or, conceivably, he might *like* giving tours of ancient bedrooms and showing the afternoon bridge club ladies how little Mary Elise Nearing in 1841 left the "Q" out of her sampler. I wanted to ask him, "What's a nice boy like you doing leading historic home tours?"

On the way downstairs again to tour the interesting buildings on the grounds my mother muttered, "I've been studying his hair, Nan. It's real."

"Did you think it was a wig?"

"For a tour like this it could have been. Sort of to match the breeches."

"I like his hair."

"The hair is fine. I would just prefer hair that long to be on a girl." Clearly Mother felt if she were in charge such things would not go on.

His hair was much longer than mine. It would be odd to date a boy with hair longer than your own. A terrible fear began rising in me and I grabbed Mother's arm. "Mother," I hissed, "don't you dare say anything to him about not liking his hair."

"Nancy, if people don't tell him their viewpoints, how will he know?"

"I'm sure he's not interested in your viewpoint."

"Nancy, he's been giving me his viewpoint for the last half hour and I intend to give him mine."

"Oh, God," I said prayerfully. But it is my experience that even God does not like to interfere with Mother when she decides to offer her viewpoint. I thought I couldn't stand it if she said anything to him. Our tour group consisted of the bridge ladies, who were giggling and gossiping with each other, and Mother and me. There was no way I could pretend not to be with Mother. And I could not stand it if she spoke to this boy. "Mother," I said firmly, "if you say anything about his long hair I will not drive you home."

Mother gaped at me. I felt quite proud of having spoken up.

The boy said, "That's okay. Somebody tells me at least once a day that I ought to get my hair cut." He was grinning at me.

I nearly died. The blush was back worse than before. After all that, *I* was the one to make the comment about his hair! I'd been so intense about reprimanding Mother I had raised my voice instead of whispering. All the bridge group was frowning at me with pursy little lips of disapproval. But they were obviously interested.

One of them said, "You really should cut your hair, you know. That phase has passed. Nobody wears it long like that now."

The boy grinned. Easily. Not a trace of a blush. "I do," he said, with complete courtesy. "Now if you would like something to drink, there's a vending machine in the barn, and bathrooms, and a pay phone. The Historical Society does not charge for the tour and would be glad to accept all donations which you may place in the wooden chest beside the barn door. Thank you for coming and I hope you enjoyed the tour."

He wound down his speech, sounding like an airline hostess demonstrating rescue equipment. Bored. Practiced.

Another bridge lady said to him, "If I make a donation, would you use it at the barbershop?"

Now if it had been me getting that kind of ribbing — smiles along with it, yet basically rude and barbed — I'd have died long since. The boy merely grinned again and said, "No, ma'am, I wouldn't. It would go to the restoration of the chestnut fences which have begun rotting in several places and need repair badly."

"Who does the repair work? You?" said my mother.

"Yes, ma'am. I also mow the lawns and weed the gardens and pick up the trash."

If I'd ever heard a line, that was one, but Mother and the bridge ladies were consoled by the thought of his doing all that hard work for such a good cause. They left him alone and went into the barn for vending machine sodas, bathrooms, and donations. The boy and I were left alone. I tried to think of something to say to him. For instance: What is your name? Do you love me too? How are we going to get together when you live one hundred and seventy miles away?

But I couldn't think of anything I could really say out loud. I wanted to say that I liked his hair, and also his costume and his grin, and the way he parried their remarks. But by the time I'd decided to frame a question about his clothes he had turned and walked away.

So that was that. Fall in love with your tour guide and off he goes to lead another tour. You're nothing but a face in the crowd.

I sighed.

Mother waylaid him. "Young man," she said.

In a very nice way he raised his eyebrows to answer her. I thought every inch of him was cute. Especially his eyebrows. What would I say to Holly? He has the cutest eyebrows, Holly. When will I ever meet anybody again with eyebrows that cute?

And yet I couldn't bring myself to ask about the Nearings. Much as I wanted his attention I really didn't want it. I wasn't close enough to stop Mother's questions. I braced myself for a long and embarrassing flow of family history. "Where is a good antique shop?" said Mother, and for once I blessed her one-track mind.

"There's one in downtown Nearing River," he began.

"You mean there's an uptown?" said Mother incredulously.

He laughed. "No. There's downtown and there's country."

"We went to the one downtown. Is there another?"

"Yes, ma'am. About two miles up the road. Nearing's Antiques and Junk."

Mother practically salivated. Not only antiques, but also junk. And some Nearings who might be alive to tell her about other Nearings, such as my father and the Nelle Catherines before me.

"Thank you," she said, but he had already gone up on the porch to lead the next tour. I looked at him for a bit but he was not thinking of me. He was trying to keep a woman from breaking off stems from the English box to plant in her own garden.

The best adjective to apply to my crush on him was "short." The only forty-five-minute love affair on record. No, it hadn't been an affair.

Affairs take two. I had been thrilled by his eyebrows but he hadn't even seen mine.

I slid behind the wheel and told Mother I didn't care *whose* antique shop it was, I had to have lunch first.

Three

It is much easier to face another antique shop when you are full of french fries, a triple burger, and a chocolate shake.

I was positively enthusiastic when I pulled our poor old car up in front of Nearing's Antiques and Junk. (Our car practically qualifies as both.) "Thank heaven," said Mother, "they didn't spell it *junque*. I like them better already."

We hopped out. I didn't roll up the windows or lock the doors; it was already hot, although it was just May, and I didn't want to get back into a cooker. I stick to the seat, and then I'm afraid to get out of the car in case I look damp around the edges.

We went in to begin poking around.

It was Mother's kind of shop. Rickety little chairs with piles of mismatched crockery on them. Sagging old photographs and odd Victorian portraits all over the walls. Torn rag rugs and pieces of quilt draped on the tops of bureaus that lacked one drawer or all knobs. A cash register as ornate as a bride's embroidery. A headboard desperately in need of refinishing and a rocker minus the cane seat. A proprietor who is middle-aged, smiling, smoking a pipe, and eager to talk antiques with other true antique hunters.

He and Mother were buddies in about sixty seconds and I could see it was going to be a long visit. It was one of the times when Mother was right that I should have a little hobby. Cross-stitch or crochet or needlepoint would be a useful sort of thing to do when Mother gets into an antique huddle. I looked for a chair that didn't have junk stacked on it, but there were none. I leaned against the least cluttered wall in the room and patiently waited. As I say, a girl fortified by french fries and so forth can be much more patient than a girl who has had nothing since breakfast.

"But that's fascinating!" caroled the man with the pipe. "But how terribly exciting! How utterly intriguing!"

I was willing to bet a tankful of gas it wasn't *that* interesting.

The man left Mother and came right over to me, took both my hands in his, and squeezed them. "Another N. C. Nearing," he said affectionately, as if we had known each other for years. And he kissed me.

I was really quite startled. I suppose if I had a father and uncles and big brothers I'd be used to that kind of kissing, but I wasn't and I jumped a foot when he did it. And then I couldn't think of anything to say — my usual verbal speed. I *think* very well; it's talking that's hard. I gave him a big uncertain smile, the kind that always makes me think of the Miss America contest when the three semifinalists have to keep on beaming, knowing that two of them are about to lose. Mother jumped into the silence. "But we don't really know if we are related to these Nearings," she said. "It was just the cookbook that gave me the idea."

"But you must be, my dear, must be. How completely intriguing. We must find out who your husband was. Let me see now. When was Robert Nearing born? What was his full name? How did you meet? What did he look like?"

Mother launched into this like a ship on her first voyage. She left out nothing, although really there was little to tell because we knew so little of Father. Mother thickened the narrative with little tales of my childhood. Mother likes to embellish her stories. *I* call it plain old lying, but Mother gets very hurt and insists that's the way it really happened, even though she never told that version before. You would not believe the tales she told this man. I kept telling myself it was all right, we would never meet him again; but the chances were that we might very well meet him again, if we really were related. And he would tell all these embarrassing stories to these other Nearings. Even before they met me they'd be laughing at me. I could visualize a big gaggle of unknown relatives bursting into laughter, saying with amusement, "So this is Nancy," and then hugging me while they repeated the silly stories. I'd never need to buy blusher because my cheeks would be permanently red.

Mother began on the tale of how I used to try

to sell her lingerie to the neighbors when I was about four and wanted to buy myself a trip to the moon with the astronauts.

The antique shop owner was laughing heartily and kept looking at me fondly. I had very mixed feelings about the whole episode.

"Robert Nearing," he said reflectively. "Unfortunately the Nearings have always tended to have enormous families. Litters, almost. I'm sure there were a number of Robert Nearings. It's not going to be easy to track him down. But it's essential, isn't it? Think of having a sixteen-year-old N. C. Nearing drop in! It really tickles me, Mrs. Nearing, it really does. You see, I happen to have a seventeen-year-old N. C. Nearing myself!"

He did not pronounce N.C. slowly, like two separate letters with periods. He said it fast and run together: Ency, so you could hear how they got Nancy from it. Ency, I thought. My name was really meant to be Ency, not Nancy. I wondered if this seventeen-year-old N. C. Nearing would be a boy or a girl. I wondered, really, which would be nicer: a girl cousin one year older, to swap stories with, try on make-up with, tell things to; or a boy cousin with whom I could be just as tongue-tied as I am with all other boys.

Of course, it hardly mattered. One hundred and seventy miles is a little far for developing close ties with people who may or may not be related.

"And so your name is Nearing, too?" said my mother excitedly.

"Yes, indeed. Dave Nearing. I'm not an Ency.

My older brother was the Ency in our generation."

"You mean they named boys N. C., too?" said Mother.

"Sure. Just as many male Encys as female Encys. Place is strewn with 'em."

I really preferred Nancy. Ency sounded peculiar. Half-baked. Rustic.

"But the boys couldn't have been Nelle Catherine," objected Mother.

"Nope. The boys' names have varied quite a bit. They just kept the initials the same. Read somewhere that crooks using aliases do that too. Get kind of a kick out of that. Anyway, some of the boys have been Nathan Clarence and Norbert Claud and Nelson Cecil."

Norbert Claud, I thought. Now that is cruel, that is truly cruel. I hope the poor thing gets called Ency instead. For him, Ency would definitely be a step up.

"You have some lovely things here," my mother said, looking around the shop.

Mr. Nearing beamed. I looked around, but I didn't see anything lovely. All I saw was a lot of junk. They began fondling a hand-carved wooden lemon squeezer and rhapsodizing over an old tobacco tin. Mother told Mr. Nearing all about how she got started in kitchen antiques and he told her all about how he got started running a shop. When he brought out a poster advertisement from the 1930's for packaged grits, Mother crooned with joy.

I took one look at the price and said, "Remember, we have to put gas in the tank to go home."

Mother was quite annoyed with me. I saw that already she was not classifying Mr. Nearing as just another antique shop owner and she didn't want him to know we had financial problems. Usually it's good to establish that because it opens the door for a little gentle dickering. Furthermore, if she did buy it at that price we really would run out of gas on some isolated road fifty miles from home. How much more loving can a daughter get?

"Hi, Dad," said a voice.

The voice sounded familiar even with as short a speech as that. It had a taped bored sound. I held my breath. Into the shop came my handsome tour guide, now wearing blue jeans, an oxford shirt with the sleeves rolled up, sneakers — and the same ponytail.

The thought that my afternoon's fantasy might actually be coming true was more frightening than anything else. I don't know why it is that when I wish for something I'm actually upset if it comes true. It was very possible that this marvelous guy was my very own cousin, and all I felt was tension. I wondered if this Ency were Norbert Claud.

"My son," said Mr. Nearing. "Ency Nearing. Don't mind his ponytail. He's not a hippie, just sort of sloppy. Ency, say hey to these nice ladies."

The boy grinned his same old nice grin. "Already did say hello, Dad. They were just on the tour. I told them to come shop here."

"You recommended somebody's else's store first," said my mother accusingly. "And this is your father's store!"

Oh no! She was going to get him in trouble before I even knew him. I cringed.

Mr. Nearing laughed. "That store's mine, too. I keep my classy stuff down there and my browsing junk up here. Here's where I do my refinishing. My sister-in-law runs the downtown store."

I was planning some pretty interesting conversation. It's always the first sentence I have trouble with. Everything after that seems to fall in place, but it's getting the first line out, without stumbling on it, that I can't manage.

"They tell you they're Nearings, too?" said Mr. Nearing. "This pretty young lady is another Ency Nearing."

How peculiar it sounded! Ency.

"No kidding," he said. He sounded as if Ency Nearings grew on every street corner and meeting another one, even one like me, was not any more interesting than the wing chair by the fireplace at the historic house.

"I pronounce it Nancy, actually," I said nervously. I rather hoped he would reveal his real name so I'd know if he were Norbert Claud.

"Glad to meet you, Nancy." When he nodded at me his ponytail quivered. He was so cute! I couldn't stand his voice, though. It still sounded rehearsed and recorded.

My mother said (I should have known she would), "Your voice sounds as if it has retreads."

His father shouted with laughter. "He always sounds like that after the Saturday tours. That's his cool, casual, competent, tour-guide voice. It'll wear off by tomorrow."

The boy flushed scarlet and gave me the puckered smile I give people when my mother embarrasses me. Our names hadn't given me any sense of kinship, but the blush did.

"Well, don't just stand there, son," said Mr. Nearing. "Start cleaning up the place."

Cleaning up? I thought. It would take a Mack truck to carry off the junk in this place.

The boy — I really couldn't call him Ency; he didn't have an Ency bone in his body — found a broom and began sweeping toward the front door. This basically had the effect of raising a lot of dust and making my mother cough. Mr. Nearing watched proudly.

"It makes him feel better about my hair," said the boy to me. "If I work I'm not a complete slouch, but a contributing member of a family with a strong work ethic."

I laughed. His voice had broken, saying that, the way boys' voices do when they're changing.

"Do you work?" he said to me.

"Sort of. I'm my mother's chauffeur. We drive all over Virginia and North Carolina antiquing."

"I don't even want to hear about it. I've spent my life in the back seat of a car between a broken chest and an antique doll without arms."

"Antique dolls?" said mother eagerly. "Broken chests?"

"Robert Nearing," murmured Mr. Nearing reflectively. "And he'd have been about my age. I can't place him. However, I had thirty-two first cousins. If he were a second, third, or fourth cousin, or over in the once-removed or twice-removed category, I could have lost track. Two decades have passed since he had any contact with any family he may have had."

Oddly enough, I couldn't seem to concentrate on their conversation. I said to the boy, "Do you like giving historic house tours?" I decided to gather all my courage and risk being really honest with whatever his name was (let it not be Norbert Claud, please). "Personally, I think when you've seen one eighteenth-century plantation house, you've seen them all."

"Oh, absolutely," he said. "And believe me, I've seen them all. I'm surprised I've never seen you before, since we've obviously spent our formative years in the same places."

I knew without doubt that if I had ever seen *him* before, I'd remember. "So your name is . . . is . . ." I couldn't quite manage Ency.

"Nick," he said. "Only my parents call me Ency. I can't wait till I leave for college and nobody knows about this N. C. Nearing jazz."

"Nick," I said, and I wanted to hug him I was so relieved. I was afraid I really would hug him, so I sort of tucked my hands around myself instead. I could *not* have told Holly that I was in love with a guy named Norbert Claud who had cute eyebrows.

"Yeah. Nicholas Charles Nearing. What did you get stuck with? Nelle Catherine?"

"Yes."

"I never minded that so much. Good thing. I have about six relatives named that."

"My goodness. How do you keep them all straight?"

"Different names and titles, basically."

"Titles?"

"Like aunt and cousin. I have an aunt Nancy, an aunt Nella, a great-aunt Cathy, a cousin

Nelle C, a cousin Ency Stewart, a cousin Catherine, and a grandmother Ency."

I could not imagine a family of such vast proportions. Mr. Nearing had thirty-two first cousins. I didn't think I even knew thirty-two people well enough to be invited to birthday parties, let alone consider them family. "And those are your relatives," I said, bemused.

Nick listened to my mother and his father talking about who Robert Nearing was. His father said, "Might be your relatives, too, Nancy. Mind the shop, Nick old boy. Mrs. Nearing and I are going out back to study my genealogy tables. We have to pin down this husband of hers. Anybody that would name his daughter Ency is a cousin of mine."

"Do they all live around here?" I asked Nick as the door shut behind our parents.

"Who?"

"All these hordes of Nearings."

"I'd say about half and half."

"Half what?"

"About half stay in the area, in this county, or in commuting distance, depending where they can get jobs, you know, and they love it. The other half flee at age eighteen, to return annually in August for reunions."

"I gather you see yourself in the fleeing half."

"I've fantasized all my life about leaving Nearing River."

I could think of a fine town up in Virginia I could offer him, but it seemed a bit premature in our relationship to mention that. "My father must have felt that way," I said. "He never told

Mother anything about his family or background."

"Maybe he had a shady past he had to escape."

"Mother would love it. She would think it was very romantic."

"Probably depend on how shady it was," said Nick. "Some shades are not romantic!"

A customer came in. Or at least, I thought it was a customer. It was a large bosomy woman who sort of rolled when she walked. There didn't seem to be room for her in the little aisles between the Nearing junk. "Hello, darling," she said. "How was school?"

"It's Saturday, Aunt Catherine. I had tours."

"Oh, yes. I do lose track of time when I work weekends. How were the tours?"

"They don't change much, Aunt Catherine. Same chimneys, same dentil molding, same wing chair."

"I knew you didn't really think that wing chair was interesting," I said.

He grinned. It made my heart spring to see that grin. This is ridiculous, I thought. Once there was this girl named Nancy who fell in love with her brand-new umpteenth cousin Nick, but they never saw each other again because they lived one hundred and seventy miles apart.

And it was a long hundred and seventy miles. I knew, having driven it. You didn't just happen by or saunter in at that distance. And I had to drive it again. I looked at my watch. It was four o'clock. We really had to get started. On the other hand, once we got started, I'd never see Nick Nearing again.

"Who's your girlfriend?" said his aunt. "Really, Nicholas, you have no manners at all. Stand up and introduce me."

"Yes, ma'am." Nick stood up. "This is a possible new cousin, Nancy Nearing. Nancy, my aunt, Mrs. Nearing."

"Nancy, my dear, what a pleasure. And what is a possible cousin, pray tell?"

I gave her our analysis of the situation and she was very interested. "My, you're a pretty girl," she said. "Though I don't see any Nearing features in you, I must admit. I wish Nick looked as decent."

"He looks fine to me," I mumbled, which was the understatement of the century.

"He," said Mrs. Nearing, with great finality, "has a ponytail." Obviously the long hair presented quite a problem to the Nearing clan. Nick's aunt turned her prow toward the back room and went to join the adults at the genealogy tables.

"I sure hope you like your ponytail," I said. "You have to pay for it daily."

"Actually," he confided, "I hate it. It's a real pain. Everybody else has short hair and the interesting part of having long hair is over. All it is now is hair hanging in my eyes."

"If you cut it, though," I said, "you'd spend all next year being congratulated for finally being decent."

He patted my shoulder. "Exactly. It's a no-win situation. I feel perfectly decent in a ponytail and now it's a matter of honor to keep it."

"How tiring to have to maintain one's honor

with a ponytail," I said, finding myself laughing helplessly.

Nick shouted with laughter, just like his father. I had this painful awful moment of wondering what my father's laugh had been like, if he had shouted that huge thick guffaw of pleasure when I was a baby and he played with me. Nick saw my expression change and he was abruptly unsure of himself. I wanted to explain what I was thinking, but just at that moment the three adult Nearings popped out of the back room. Aunt Catherine walked in first, as though her bulk had to be shoveled out before the others could fit. "Sell anything, Ency?" said Nick's father.

"No, Dad. Nobody came in."

"Well, close up shop. We're going home."

I stood up and tried to think of something witty to say in farewell. It was complicated by the fact that I was feeling tearful for the father I had never known. It seemed so unfair that these people had a huge family they took for granted while I had none. It was the first time I had ever felt sad about Father. The shouts of laughter, identical in father and son, had done it. "Good-bye," I said, with great originality. "It's been nice talking to you."

"Save the good-byes," said Mr. Nearing. "We haven't figured out yet who your father is, Nancy, and I am determined to get to the bottom of this."

"We're going to the Nearings' for dinner," said Mother, who was absolutely beaming and flushed and excited. A clear overdose of antiquery.

"But Mother," I said. "It's such a long drive home and it'll be after dark and — "

"Nonsense," said Aunt Catherine. "I made enough Brunswick stew for an army. The house is just back of the store behind that poplar hedge. Delighted to have you. No trouble, no trouble at all. Hope you have a big appetite. I can't stand people who don't eat."

Nick was already bringing the antiques that had been displayed outside back into the shop. Pretty soon the narrow aisles were impassable. We sort of backed out of the store through the genealogy room, which was nothing but a shed with a desk and some books. We walked through the parking area, which was red clay with a few token pebbles on it.

"Nick, you and your new cousin bring her car. Mrs. Nearing is walking back with Aunt Catherine and me."

Nick said, "Dad, I'm going to the high school musical tonight, remember? I mean, I'm glad to drive the car over, but — "

But he had plans, he meant. Don't rope me into an evening entertaining some new cousin, Dad, is what he meant. I said hastily, "I'm the chauffeur, remember? You go on to your show."

"No, no, I didn't mean that, Nancy. The show isn't till eight, I have loads of time. Dad forgets things and I have to keep nagging. Once they get started talking genealogy they can go on for hours at a time and I'm never excused because they think it's good for me to be exposed to family ties. Okay. You chauffeur me." He hopped into Mother's seat, and it was most odd to have someone other than Mother sitting there. I wouldn't be half as good a driver if Nick were my passenger. The traffic would be far less interesting.

We drove the few hundred yards to his house, which was not historical or plantation at all, but brick split-level. "Will this bother your mother?" I said. "Having us drop in like this?"

"Mom and Dad are divorced. She didn't like being overwhelmed by Nearings. She says it was like being married to a clan instead of a man. She lives in Pennsylvania. I spend Christmas and all of July with her. Aunt Catherine lives with us."

He sounded very matter-of-fact about it, but then, I sound very matter-of-fact about my father being dead all these years. I parked the car and we got out. Nick rolled up his window and went around and rolled up mine and said, "Got your keys?" and when I said I did, he locked the doors.

I must have looked surprised because he said, "A rash of robberies lately. Way out here in the boondocks. Doesn't seem very neighborly, does it? We have to be pretty careful."

We went up to the porch and he took my elbow and said, "The lower step is rickety. I have to replace it and I keep forgetting. Careful."

I felt like Cinderella at the ball. My elbow actually felt special. Good grief, girl, I told myself, get a grip on yourself.

I walked in to face Aunt Catherine's Brunswick stew. I *hate* Brunswick stew. Obviously, though, a new cousin just invited by her new aunt for a home-prepared meal does not say "Yuck!" when handed a plate.

"I hate Brunswick stew," said Nick. "If you

want to have a peanut butter and jelly sandwich with me, Nancy, I'll make you one, too."

Which is how Nick and I ended up in the kitchen talking while Mother and the new Nearings sat in the dining room working their way through genealogy and antiques.

Four

"I," said Nick, "am a peanut butter freak. Likewise a jam connoisseur. In peanut butter, I am featuring crunchy, smooth, old-fashioned stir-from-the-bottom, and Aunt Catherine's homemade blender peanut butter from Uncle Norbert's own peanuts. In jam I am offering Aunt Catherine's own grape, red plum, hot pepper, and plain old strawberry."

"Did you say hot pepper jam?"

"Actually it's jelly. It's peculiar. Usually you eat it with cream cheese on a cracker, I don't know why."

"What's it taste like? Spicy?"

"No. Sort of tangy and strange. Sometimes I like it and mostly I don't. Hot pepper jelly is a local specialty. I feel sure there was an Ency Nearing recipe for it in that cookbook."

"No doubt. Could I try a speck of hot pepper jelly and cream cheese on a cracker, but really have Aunt Catherine's homemade blender peanut butter from Uncle Norbert's own peanuts with plain old strawberry jam?"

"A girl of sense. Certainly. Will you have this sandwich on white or Aunt Catherine's own health loaf?"

"Aunt Catherine seems to do a lot of cooking."

"What she mostly does," said Nick, grinning again, "is eating."

I decided on her health bread, and it was a very tasty choice. Nick sliced off pieces so thick I could hardly fit my mouth around the sandwich. I felt like Heidi on the mountain or something, eating my cottage-made goodies. The trouble with the kind of chewing I had to do was that I felt very conspicuous opening my mouth as wide as a whale's jaws to fit it in. Nick seemed to be able to eat very neatly. My whole end of the table was a mess of crumbs and jam.

Nick furthermore was able to talk neatly, courteously, and very articulately with his mouth full. When I have a mouth full of peanut butter and jelly I can hardly even move my tongue. So he would deliver these long involved treatises with strings of adjectives and phrases and I would go "urhgoomph" and try to swallow.

And all the time I thought how marvelously cute he was. I really did like his eyebrows best. When he grinned his eyebrows would lift first, like a signal, and then the grin would zip around his face. "Do you cook, too," I said, "or are you chiefly a sandwich-maker?"

"I have to clean up. Sometimes I have very mixed feelings when Aunt Catherine goes on a baking binge. The results are terrific but I hate to walk in here and see seven muffin tins and eleven cooky sheets and flour all over the floor and butter in the sink. I hate scouring pans."

"My own personal life desire," I said, "is to be able to eat all my meals out."

"I don't know. I like it both ways. I'd like to alternate meals, I think. Aunt Catherine's cooking for supper, breakfast at McDonald's, Aunt Catherine's sandwiches, supper at the Steak House, and so on."

"You'd still have to do an awful lot of cleaning up."

"I know. Haven't ever figured out a way around housework. And believe me, I've tried. My cousin Roy's wife says a clean house is a sign of a misspent life."

"She should visit us. She'd definitely feel we'd spent ours well."

"Antiques do gather dust, don't they?"

"You must look forward to going to Pennsylvania, Nick. No more kitchen chores there, huh?"

"Heck, no, it's worse there. My mom is convinced I'm going to grow up to be a complete male chauvinist pig. She thinks one day I'll get so sick of dishes and laundry I'll get married just in order to find somebody else to do the dishes and laundry."

"I'm sure it's tempting. I'd get married in a second if I thought my husband would do all the dishes and laundry."

We laughed.

"Anyway," said Nick, "Mom feels the only way to endure housekeeping is to share it. And since she does it all year except Christmas and July, she figures my share is around the clock when I do visit. The only thing I know for sure about Pennsylvania is the price of linoleum shiner."

How typical, I thought, how annoying, that my only conversation with a marvelous boy is the exact same conversation I'd have with my mother: dishes, kitchen, laundry, and chores.

Nick finished eating first, cleared the table, and slid the dishes into a plastic pan full of soapy water. He put away the jam and peanut butter, mopped up my mess, and went in to clear off the grown-ups' table.

We talked and talked and talked while doing the dishes. I even told Nick why I'd gotten upset when he burst out laughing in the store, that I was thinking about my father's laugh and what it was like and how I'd never heard it.

"I guess it's good for me to hear you talk like that," said Nick. "I get so sick of family, family, family. I shouldn't take them for granted, I suppose."

"I don't see how you can take family for granted when your parents are divorced." As soon as I said that I was horrified at myself. It was an awfully personal remark to make to somebody I barely knew. And a little rude, too.

Nick just smiled a little. "I guess you're right, I don't really take it for granted. My visits to Mom always include an exchange where she lectures me about sharing. Sharing chores, sharing cooking, sharing thoughts, and so forth. And I always ask her how come she doesn't come back home and share a little bit with Dad and me. And then she loses her temper and stomps off."

"What do you do when you visit her? Take lots of neat trips? Sit around talking? Or what?"

"We used to go camping a lot. Mom loves camping and hiking. But she has a pretty demanding job now and she only takes a week's vacation, so we camp that week and the rest of July I just hang around. I'm not going to go up this year, actually. I haven't told her that yet. I'm not looking forward to that phone call, I can tell you."

"How come you're not going?"

"Well, this sounds terrible, and I guess maybe it is terrible, but I have better things to do. I have two jobs lined up for summer." He grinned at me. "Both of them beat antique house tours by a mile."

"Tell me." I hadn't been able to find a job yet that Mother would let me take. The only one available was nights at a twenty-four hour Quik-Stop store, and Mother was convinced it would be robbed while I was alone there.

"I'm going to be working from seven A.M. till three P.M. at the hospital as a janitor in the emergency ward and Thursday, Friday, and Saturday nights I'm at the roller rink fitting roller skates."

I laughed. "I love skating. Do you?"

"I can't do it," he admitted. "I've never managed to do anything like that. I can't skate or ski, or even skateboard. I have a rotten sense of balance. But for this job it doesn't matter. I just get out the skates and help the little kids lace them up and so forth. It pays pretty well and I really need the money. I'll never get to college if I don't get my act together and start saving."

We talked about college and jobs and life and families and once I said something that Nick agreed with so much he actually lifted his Coke and clicked it against mine to toast me.

There is a word I came upon in my reading of paperback historical romances, although I have never heard anyone actually use the word out loud. Besotted. It feels very Middle Ages, and the idea of it is that everybody is hanging around in the castle hall drinking too much at the same time they're falling in love — so they feel as if they're almost too much in love!

I was pretty sure I was well on the road to being besotted.

From the dining room came my mother's triumphant "Ah ha!" followed quickly by Aunt Catherine's "Well, I swan!" and Mr. Nearing's "Eureka!"

"Gold?" said Nick. "Silver?"

"No," called his father. "The missing Robert Nearing."

I rushed into the dining room to see what they had discovered. Spread out on the table — reaching from the end where the place mats and napkins were stacked to the opposite rim where the three people hovered — were genealogy tables written in tiny pinched letters on hand-drawn lines. Obviously, with as many children as all those Nearings had chosen to have, mass-produced genealogy charts allowing for two offspring were not very useful. I squinted at the tables. Way off at one side was a Robert Nearing, squished between one N.C. Nearing, one Rosemary Nearing m. Cal Stewart, one Lucy Nearing m. Ben Ransom (Rosemary and Lucy both had five children), and two more brothers whose names I could not make out. "So who is he?" I said.

"Well, my grandfather David Nearing's sister Lucy married her fourth cousin Peter Nearing, and their son Matthew married his second cousin Catherine Nearing who had a son by a first marriage that Matthew adopted, and he —" Mr. Nearing's face fell. "Oh no. I've got my sheets mixed up." He realigned two of his pages. "There we go." Everybody scrunched down to stare. It would have been easier if Aunt Catherine had not taken up so much more than her fair share of the space. "Now," said Nick's father. "This Robert's father is Hartwell Nearing, the third son of Glory Fairchild and Evan Nearing, who is not Matthew's adopted son after all, but —"

"No," said Aunt Catherine, "you're wrong. I remember Hartwell's boys. Robert was my age and he was killed in Korea."

"Nonsense. That was Marcus," said Mr. Nearing.

"Call Glory," said Aunt Catherine, "it's her grandson."

"You're right," he said, changing sides immediately. "Glory hasn't got any missing grandsons. Do I have my sheets in the right order?"

Nick said, "Well, Nancy, it's been nice meeting you. Enjoyed talking and all. I've got to run if I'm going to get to the play in time. See you."

His father was muttering to himself. "Great-great-grandfather Marcus had seven sons, and the truth is that my great-uncle Lawson went to live in Washington state and we've completely lost track of him. He could have had scads of offspring."

I said, "Thank you for making me a sandwich, Nick" and he said, "No problem," and went off with his ponytail swinging, pounding up the half-stairs to the bedroom end of the split-level.

I went into the living room. Mr. Nearing's specialty was Carolina country furniture. Everything was very old, dark, marred, and rather crudely made. It had a certain utilitarian beauty, although I myself want a house, someday, furnished in all upholstered things with lots of chrome and glass and wall-to-wall carpet. On the hardwood floors of this living room were a dozen or more rag rugs, scattered awkwardly, even treacherously, and all of them looked a little too old to be walked on. I chose a rocker and sat down gingerly, but the chair creaked so ominously I lifted myself out of it without exerting any more pressure on it. I went back into the kitchen, where the chairs were sturdy thick things from the Sears catalog.

I sighed. The adults' conversation in the dining room was almost intolerable. The drive back home to Virginia seemed impossibly long, something I could never undertake. I began twirling a spoon Nick had forgotten to put away.

I decided to prod Mother along. Mr. Nearing and Aunt Catherine came into the kitchen to use the phone as I went back to the dining table. He began a complex conversation with somebody about the Ransom Nearing branch of the family. Aunt Catherine interrupted to say she remembered Connie's baby perfectly and that he had gone to live in Colorado where he married somebody or other. My mother said, "Oh, Nancy, this is so exciting. Do you realize we may actually find some family for you? My, my, look at this bunch over here. Eleven children, and each one of them married, and the smallest family anyone had was six children, and all but three of them survived to have children, and that's still two generations before Bob's!"

I sat on the bottom step of the stairs and pleated my fingers in front of my face and worried about driving home in the dark. Headlights blind me. Roads without white lines terrify me. What if we got lost and drove forever in rural North Carolina?

"Uh, Nancy?" said Nick. "May I get by?"

I jumped up, flustered, and stepped on his sneaker. "Oh, I'm sorry. Are you all right, Nick?"

"Sure. Tough toes run in the Nearing family."

"Nancy," said his father, "why don't you go with Nick to this performance? It's Gilbert and Sullivan. *The Mikado.* That way your mother and I can fuss over this for another few hours without worrying about how bored you're getting."

Nick looked as if his father had hit him. I thought of all the easy grins he'd given all day long. Here he had to spend time in public with me and he couldn't summon one up. I said quickly, "I'd love that, but we have a four-hour drive ahead of us and we need to get started, don't we, Mother?"

"I don't see why. I'm not tired. I'll drive home, Nancy, you go on with Nick."

It was obviously fine with everybody but Nick.

His Aunt Catherine said, "Take my jeep, Nick, it's not filled up with antiques like your father's van. He forgot to unload it this morning after that auction."

I said, "No, Nick, that's okay. I brought a paperback along. I don't want to impose on you."

"Impose!" snorted his father. "Nick will have a fine time. Go along, you two."

Nick hauled out a smile that made me flush almost painfully. It was very much an obedient, doing-my-duty smile. "I think it'll be a pretty good show, Nancy. And you can meet some more cousins. Another Ency Nearing is the Lord High Executioner and my second cousin Sue Stewart is Yum Yum."

My mother howled with laughter. "Nancy, what icing on the cake!" she chortled. "Cousins who are Lord High Executioner and Yum Yum. Have a good time, dear."

"I wanted Nick to be in it," said his father, "seeing as how he's the only boy in the high school who already has a ponytail. The ones who are in the Chinamen chorus had to have 'em glued on. But he flunked the audition. Can't match pitch. Even Gilbert and Sullivan requires that much."

Nick's smile was very tight. "Well, cousin," he said to me, taking my arm, "let's go. If I hear much more talk about my hair I'll turn violent, so we'd better hurry."

We clattered out the back door and hurried to the jeep parked out under some trees. Nick started the engine as if he were starting a war.

We drove in complete silence the several miles to the school. All the time I wanted to jump out of the jeep, or apologize to him for being foisted off on him. But I was afraid I would burst into tears because I felt so awful about it, so I didn't say anything at all.

Five

We came to a red light and Nick stopped. The jeep was not particularly comfortable, although it was sort of neat to be sitting in one, with the little plastic zipped-up sides and doors and windows. I said, "It seems odd that your Aunt Catherine drives a jeep."

"Listen, if she felt like it, Aunt Catherine could drive a herd of cattle."

I tried to laugh, but Nick almost sounded as if he were yelling at me, so I just looked out the window instead.

We pulled into the high school parking lot. Usually I vault out of a car the instant it stops, but this time I just sat there, trying to tell myself that everything would be okay, that I could get through the evening all right, that I'd be fine no matter how humiliating it was, that it would probably give me more poise — and so forth. By the time I'd finished thinking all that, Nick had walked around and opened my door for me. Obviously it irritated him, that I was treating the evening like a date while for him it was an unwanted chore.

A boy and a girl got out of a Chrysler K car next to us, a lovely, brand-new, sparkling white model, and they both shouted. "Nicholas Nearing on a date! I don't believe it," said the boy. "Will wonders never cease."

The girl was laughing. "About time, Nick. Introduce us."

Nick said through his teeth, "This is just another cousin of mine. Nancy Nearing, this is Julie Hume and the jerk over there is Ben Earl."

We barely had time to exchange hellos, because Nick was leaving for the auditorium and I had to trot after him. "Nick!" yelled a pair of boys. They loped over to us, grinning from ear to ear. "Who's your girlfriend?"

"This," said Nick emphatically, "is my cousin." He did not introduce us. We strode on past them toward the foyer of the auditorium.

There must have been seventy-five people milling around in there who were related to Nick and another two hundred who were not but who knew him. Shouting, gossiping, teasing, alternately admiring the artwork on the foyer walls and telling Nick they had thought he'd never start dating — it was a nightmare for both of us. My cheeks were so red I felt as if I were made up like a clown with red spots for cheeks. "Nick, a girlfriend at last. Introduce us." "Say, you got a cute one when you finally got one." "What's the matter, Nick, townies not good enough for you? Have to go out of the state to get a girl?"

And each time Nick would glue on his tight little smile (such an embarrassing contrast to his beautiful easy grin) and say, "No, this is just another cousin. Nancy Nearing. Robert's daughter. They live up in Virginia. Visiting for a day." There were even a few people who claimed the world was not big enough for another Nancy Nearing and several who exclaimed, "*Robert*'s daughter! And how is Robert these days?" and then I'd have to explain that the Robert they were thinking of was not my father. Nick dragged me through the crush and finally we reached the auditorium, where Nick fell into a seat as if he'd been on his feet for several years.

"I'm sorry," I said, "I'm really sorry. I didn't mean to start all that for you. Life is bad enough with all their remarks about your hair, I'm sure. Now you have to deny all this girlfriend stuff. I'm really sorry."

He slumped way down in his seat. "Aw, it's not your fault. Actually, I feel stupid about it. It's just that everybody I know has partied and gone out for years and for some reason I'm not allowed to be quietly alone, they have to kid me about it all the time. Endlessly. I just don't . . . I haven't . . . I mean, I don't —"

"Date," I said.

"Right."

"Well, neither do I," I said, hoping to help him relax about it.

He was completely astonished. "You don't?"

"No."

"Really? Why not?"

There was only one answer to that. "I don't get asked." It sort of amused me that he couldn't understand why he got plagued over not dating. There was no doubt in my mind he'd be the number one choice of every girl in the high school. "Why don't you date?" I said.

"I hate asking," he said. "No, that's not quite right. I never *have* asked anyone out. What I hate is thinking about what it would be like to ask a girl out."

"But if you can talk so easily to me," I protested, "it should be no problem at all to call up some girl or meet her after class or something and talk to her, too."

He waved that off. "That's different. You're not a regular girl, you're a cousin. I never have trouble talking with relatives. But I don't want to ask my cousins out, you know, that way I'd never get away from family. And besides, everybody would know everything. The girl cousin would tell her other girl cousins about every kiss and every sentence and they'd tell their mothers and pretty soon the entire Nearing clan would be right on top of it. When I date it's going to be private. Actually, I'm waiting for college."

Oh brother, I thought, so much for my fantasies. Time to shelve each one of them. I found myself actually patting his hand in sympathy, and he was right; it really was very easy to get along with someone who wasn't "a regular boy," but a cousin. No stiffness between us at all.

"I know exactly why your father left and never came back, Nancy," he told me half seriously.

"Why?"

"He was drowning in relatives. The way I see it, he had been thinking for years of leaving never to return. And then one day he hiccuped in church, or some such thing, and after the service fifty-five relatives said, 'Oh, that was Robert hiccuping, I'd know his hiccup anywhere.' So Robert decided to go where he could hiccup in peace."

The image of my unknown father gratefully leaving the state in order to sit alone and hiccup was impossible. Nick and I began giggling. To prove to me how overrun he was by family, he took the program and began pointing out relatives in the cast, orchestra, chorus; doing lighting, costumes, advertising, and so forth. I realized he didn't actually know his precise relationship to most of these kids, just that he was related by blood at some point in some way. "Heck, who knows?" he said of one senior girl. "She could be an aunt for all I know. She's a Nearing somehow. You'll know her because she's the only Chinese princess with curly red hair."

Two boys sat behind us and ruined everything by making wisecracks. "What you Nearings need is a Lord High Executioner of your own," said one of them. "There are too darn many of you around."

"I'll drink to that," said Nick.

And then, to my relief, the curtain went up on *The Mikado.*

Gilbert and Sullivan, of course, is just plain fun. The leads and chorus had really good diction, so we could understand all the silly lines. The best lead by far was Ency Nearing, the Lord High Executioner. He was very tall and thin and kind of wavy, as if he had not yet made up his mind about anything in life, including his personality.

"I have a little list," he sang, "they'd none of them be missed. All people who have flabby hands and irritating laughs, they'd none of them be missed."

Nick sang in my ear, "All people who make snide remarks about my ponytail, they'd none of them be missed."

The woman in front of us turned around furiously and said, "Ssssshhh."

"You'd none of you be missed," Nick breathed at her.

I stepped on his sneaker again and he stepped back on mine and we kept this up all during the next chorus.

And the very first thing the boys behind us said when intermission came was, "Uh huh. Trying to pass her off as a cousin, Nick." "We saw you guys. You can't fool us."

"Cousin," I said firmly. "Strictly cousin. I gather you two aren't also related to me?"

Loudly they thanked God that they were not related to Nicholas Nearing.

The woman in front of us said, "Your manners, I see, Nicholas, have not improved."

Nick stood up instantly. "Mrs. Dixon, my cousin, Nancy Nearing. Nance, Mrs. Dixon, she's an English teacher."

"Another Nearing!" said Mrs. Dixon. "Honestly, Nicholas. Why don't you people contribute now and then to zero population growth?"

"We do," said Nick. "Neither Nancy nor I am a parent."

Mrs. Dixon laughed. I blushed again. Mrs. Dixon's friend said, "Really, Nick, when are you going to cut that awful hair?"

"When I go to college," said Nick, who, I was beginning to gather, looked on college as the rainbow in a life of rain.

"Oh my, is that a promise, Nick?" "How wonderful. Maybe we can get you early acceptance." "Would you like to skip your senior year in high school?" All this from the boys behind us.

"He needs that senior year," sniffed Mrs. Dixon. "His maturation level is not what it ought to be."

I could not imagine having so many people so actively interested in what I was doing. Aside from my mother, the mothers of two or three very close friends, a few teachers, and one or two neighbors, I could think of nobody who really noticed much about me, let alone expressed concern, opinions, and advice.

Eventually, all these adults and teens drifted into the foyer for drinks, bathroom, cigarettes, and gossip. We stayed quietly in our seats, by unspoken agreement not wanting to subject ourselves to that again. "Whew!" I said.

"And you wonder why I'd like to leave Nearing River?"

"No, I guess I don't wonder anymore. You must detest some of these relatives. They nag and interfere and poke fun. I don't know how you stand it."

"I guess because I'm heading into the downhill stretch. One more month of school, then summer, then my senior year, and then I'll be gone, Nancy." He said it dreamily.

"Never to return?" I asked him.

"Oh no, I like my family better than that. Or most of them. I just want them in smaller doses."

Just at that moment, an aunt to whom I'd been introduced in the lobby appeared beside us. She smiled wickedly. "As we would like to see *you* in smaller doses, Nick."

He made a face at her.

"I'm just kidding, honey," she said, "you know that. Now I've been thinking all through *The Mikado* that I really can't remember who Robert is. Now exactly whose parents are Robert's?"

And by the time we had explained that once more, intermission was over.

After the show we got surrounded by Nick's high school friends demanding that he bring his girlfriend down to Shoney's for strawberry pie along with everybody else. "My cousin," Nick kept explaining, "she's just a cousin. I'm showing her around."

His tone of voice added, Father's orders.

"Nope, can't go to Shoney's," he said several times. I wondered what Shoney's was. Obviously everybody went there. "Nancy's got to get back home, she's got a long drive ahead of her. See you guys Monday," he said.

I didn't mind as much as I'd expected. We were friends, at least, and Nick had admitted he could talk to me more easily than with any other girl. Regular girl. What an awful description.

The girl cousins to whom I was introduced — three of them within a few years of my age — actually hugged me in a welcoming greeting that made me sort of ache to be really and truly a part of the Nearing clan instead of a mere passerby. "I hope we see you again," said one of them, and she seemed to mean it. I wondered if Nick would say it. Probably not. One thing he definitely didn't want to see again was another N. C. Nearing.

We drove home talking nonstop about the pros and cons of a huge devoted family. "It's so confining," said Nick. "I don't want to be the latest in a string of N.C. Nearings. There are so many of us I'd be indistinguishable if it weren't for my ponytail."

The closest I could come to understanding that was that once in a Brownie troop there had been three girls named Nancy.

"Around here," said Nick, "it's like a tidal wave of Nearings."

"But most of them weren't even named Nearing, Nick."

"Well, no, of course not. All the women have other names. We have generations of Stewarts, Hineses, Lawsons, Harringtons, Channings — and they're all Nearings."

And then we were back at his house and our companionship was over.

In the kitchen the three adults were having, of all things, hot chocolate, sitting at the table exchanging stories.

"We didn't find your father," said Mother. "We examined every Robert on these pages and none of them matched up."

"But they'd have to," said Nick. "What about being named Nelle Catherine and called Nancy? That's no coincidence."

"No, almost certainly not," agreed his father. "But you see, the usual technique in genealogy is to work backward from the person who interests you. In other words, take Robert Nearing, move through his parents and grandparents and so forth until you bump into common relatives. Since we don't know his parents we have to start at the other direction which is hardly ever very successful. In spite of all the Nearings you swim in, son, the majority of them have always moved away. That's what settled America."

"Yeah," said Nick. "The very progeny of the Nearing clan moving westward." He made himself into a wave undulating across the house.

"It isn't funny, Ency," said his aunt. I *loathed* hearing him called that. I wondered if he did, too, but I couldn't see his expression. "Anyway, Nancy," she said, "there are generations and generations of cousinly kin about whom we know nothing and probably never will."

"My theory is," said Mother, "that he may actually have been an orphan. His parents died young or something, and he really didn't have any family but he vaguely remembered their stories. He used the name Nelle Catherine to tie his daughter to a past he really knew nothing of."

We went through a long series of exchanges on Aunt Catherine's fine Brunswick stew, Nick's excellent peanut butter and jelly sandwiches, the pleasure of each other's company, the surprise of the whole meeting.

There were comments to make on hospitality, antiques, the weather, and driving safely, and then we were all calling, "Good-bye, nice to have met you, thanks again."

Somehow I was in the driver's seat after all, and Mother on the passenger side, and Mr. Nearing was slamming the car door and going back into his house and Nick was nowhere to be seen and I was driving away.

And that was that.

Six

"Oh, Nannie," said Holly. "And you'll never see him again. How utterly romantic."

I choked on a long thread of spaghetti. "Tell me one thing romantic about *not* seeing him again," I demanded.

Holly was eating cottage cheese and applesauce. Every morning at eleven I am determined to eat the salad plate but when I get to the cafeteria line I always end up with a loaded tray. Holly put an eighth of a teaspoon of food into her mouth and said, "It's very bookish, Nan. The heroine shuts herself in her lacy boudoir to weep for the fine figure of a man she'll never be able to marry."

Ginger crunched through an apple and said juicily, "However, in books, the reason for never being able to marry is always conquered, with the insane wife dying, or the blackmailer meeting his just end, or the inheritance coming just in time. But this time the reason won't go away.

He'll always be her cousin and he'll always be one hundred and seventy miles away."

"I'm not thinking of marrying him," I said crossly. "I'd just like to have a boyfriend. And there's nothing romantic about an absentee boyfriend."

"Especially when he doesn't consider you to be a regular girl," agreed Ginger. "I consider that the remark of a skunk."

"He wasn't a skunk."

"Laura Burns's boyfriend is at college," said Holly, partaking of another two calories, "and you think that's romantic."

"Yes, but he knows he's her boyfriend and he writes to her and calls her up and she visits him on weekends. Nick does not know he is, or could be, or ought to want to be, my boyfriend."

"A tedious situation," said Ginger. She aimed her apple core at the wastebasket and hit a sophomore boy in the cheek. I speedily removed myself from the table because the sophomore clearly intended to retaliate with a plate of spaghetti. For once I was glad when the cafeteria monitor intervened, hauling poor clumsy Ginger off to the vice principal's office to explain this aggressive behavior. Holly and I cleared the table, stuck her apple core in the trash, and tagged after her in case character references were in order.

"Write to Nick," Holly suggested.

"Holly, I haven't written a letter in my life except in fourth grade when we had to study where to put the inside address and how to phrase a complimentary closing. I've never even licked a stamp."

"That's impossible. How do you pay your bills? What do you do about Christmas thank you notes to relatives in Seattle? Or letters to your congressman? Dear departed friends who jumped rope with you in fourth grade and are now living in Boston? Jewelry that is absolutely perfect and you can only get it by mail order?"

Holly was finally struck dumb when she grasped the extent of my non-letter writing. She kept shaking her head at me. Considering how few calories she ran her slender body on, I thought it remarkable she had the energy to shake it so often. "Never licked a stamp," she said. "How old are you, anyway?"

"Sixteen."

"And you've never even done volunteer work where they had mailings?"

"In all my volunteer work they've used the phone."

We sat down on the redwood picnic bench that decorates the hall outside the vice principal's office. It's where offenders wait to find out the punishment for their offenses. I had never sat there. The looks we got from kids we knew walking by were priceless. It was interesting that nobody stopped to speak to us and ask why we were there. They obviously wanted no conversation with girls who had joined the criminal element.

"Well," I said defensively, "how many letters have you ever written, Holly?"

She meditated. "Every Christmas I have thank you letters to my cousins in — "

"Skip the thank you notes. Besides them."

"Hmmm. I write my grandmother Beale every other week. I had a friend named Annie Wood back in elementary and we've written every month since she moved to Canada. I got a pen pal through a magazine once. She lived in Australia and her name was Patricia Woolley and we wrote about ten times until Patricia got a better pen pal."

"A better pen pal!" I exclaimed. "How do you know that's why she stopped writing?"

"She told me. She wrote, Dear Holly, I have now found a more interesting pen pal who lives in New York City and since I'd rather visit New York someday than Virginia and since I can't afford postage to both of you, I'm not writing to you anymore. Thanks anyway. Love, Patricia."

"Now that was low," I said.

"I didn't mind. I'm pretty sure she'd already told me everything she knew about Australia. But if you think you're getting me off the subject, you're mistaken. You should write to this Nicholas."

"I wouldn't know what to say."

"You get straight A's in English comp. You could write a good letter. I have faith in you."

"Actually I usually get A-minus."

"That's good enough for a letter. Really, Nan, I think you should thank him for taking you to the operetta. For introducing you to all those lovely people who might be your cousins. End up with a witty line about loving his ponytail and for him not to cut it off until you get there to share the big moment with him."

I could not imagine writing such a thing. Just imagining Nick opening a letter like that, and reading it, made me blush.

Ginger came out of the vice principal's office looking hunched and beaten. "What'd you get?" said Holly. "Forty lashes?"

"He just told me in the future I am to transport my apple cores in a more sedate manner. I humbly promised so to do."

We giggled, and then the second lunch bell rang and we had to scurry off to our classes. We have only a two-and-a-half minute passing period and only the luckiest can saunter, those whose classes happen to be next door. The rest of us have to charge up two flights of stairs or chug down nine corridors. (Going to the bathroom is a luxury.) I clutched my books to my chest like a battering ram and launched myself through the crowds to the basement and history.

I went into history feeling pretty good. Talking things over with your best friend always loosens things up. Holly and I hadn't resolved anything by talking about Nick and how I'd never see him again, but at least I felt more cheerful about it.

And in history the teacher passed out an exam.

I had completely forgotten about it. Completely. Friday night Mother and I spent watching movies on cable television, and of course Saturday was our Nicholas–antique–operetta night and we didn't get home till after three A.M. Sunday I slept very late, and we had brunch and lazed around talking, and Mother got out an old knitting project (she keeps old-fashioned wooden needles and twisted natural wool skeins in an antique basket by the Shaker rocker, but that's just to look good — she really knits with acrylic on steel needles). I picked up my cross-stitch and we went to bed early.

I never even glanced at my history. I never even *thought* about my history.

It was one of those awful, cruel essay tests: only two questions. I like true-false, fill in the blanks, matching columns or one sentence answers. I hate essays. In an essay, you can't guess; you have to know.

In about thirty seconds I had a fierce headache and my stomach was in knots. I just didn't know enough about either question to answer them. I felt myself beginning to cry and despised myself for it. Other people never seem to get so worked up about quizzes. Win a few, lose a few. I seem to be the only one who can cry herself to sleep over a terrible job on a test. It's so humiliating.

We once read a wonderful essay by Winston Churchill about taking his entrance exams for a British boarding school, in which the only thing he could manage to do was number the page. First he wrote a 1. Then he put a period after the 1. Then he enclosed it in parentheses. And that was all he wrote.

He got to be Prime Minister, but I was going to be a prime failure if I couldn't think of something to say about the rising wave of conservatism in the United States and how it is manifested. I thought of writing, "In my house, we manifest our conservatism by collecting kitchen antiques," but I didn't think Mr. Kane would be amused.

I wrote down some notes but they seemed irrelevant. The minutes ticked inexorably by.

Everybody else was filling in reams of paper. Two people actually asked for more paper. All I could think of was the funny door handle of Nick's jeep and the way Mrs. Dixon's auditorium seat creaked when she laughed and the hugs from the possible girl cousins and Nick's raspy cheek I'd never touched.

In the end I had to submit my test practically blank. Mr. Kane gave me a very odd look, but I managed not to cry and I fled from the room.

The problem was that I had liked Nicholas Nearing too much. Stumbling into possible relatives is emotional enough without falling in love with one of them. Really, Ginger was right. It was tedious.

I am normally quite self-disciplined. When the time comes that I absolutely can't postpone doing my paper on Lord Byron another minute, I say to myself, "Nelle Catherine, shape up and get to work." And I do. I almost never have late homework — and forgetting a history test was a first.

But that night, in spite of forty-eight algebra problems, a long French translation, and a chapter in biology to read, I sat at my desk and tried to compose a letter to Nick. "Dear Nick," I wrote.

Mother popped in. "Listen to this, Nannie. Did you happen to read this when you went through the cookbook? Our cookbook? It's a little dedicatory poem. It says — "

"Mother, really. I have homework to do."

"You're not doing homework, you're writing a letter. Listen.

'Cooks will find their labor less confusing
Whilst preparing viands succulently good
By selecting for their daily using
Nearing River's recipes for food.' "

"Magnificent," I said.

"Who are you writing to?" said Mother. "I can't ever remember you writing a letter before."

I covered the Dear Nick with my hand. "To whom am I writing?" I corrected her.

"Whatever. Whom? Whom, then?"

"Nobody, just practicing."

"Oh. That reminds me. I have to write to David and Catherine and thank them for their hospitality. They were so nice to us. Really, I don't know when I've met nicer people."

Second that, I thought.

I pulled out my algebra. Nelle Catherine, I said to myself, forget about Nicholas Charles. And his eyebrows. And his grin. And his taped voice. And his funny remarks. And his silly ponytail.

It was remarkable what a long list I had about a boy I barely knew. Here I was in school with boys I'd known all my life and I could not have listed one thing about most of them. I felt as if I knew Nick intimately — yet not at all.

I put my mind on algebraic formulas and removed N.C. Nearing from my mind. If *ax* squared plus *bx* plus *c* equals seventy-two . . .

"Thank you for taking me to *The Mikado*," I wrote. Boy, did that sound stilted. I wrote on a fresh sheet, "Dear Nick, What a good time I had with you Saturday." It sounded worse.

My mother came back in. "Listen to this, Nan.

An advertiser on the back pages of the cookbook says, 'Beware of Flavoring Extracts peddled from house to house claiming to be equal to McMonagle & Rogers' Premium Vanilla. Our thousand dollar guarantee — ' "

"Mother, please, I'm trying to do my math."

"Oh, all right." Mother straggled back out.

I remembered that the rubber band holding Nick's hair in the ponytail was red.

Good grief, I thought. I have already failed a history exam and I have this huge algebra assignment and I'm fantasizing about the rubber band in his hair.

I got down to business.

I wrote, "Dear Nick — "

Seven

In June our car died.

It was not a spectacular or speedy death. The poor old thing just began sputtering in the mornings and choking in the evenings. We kept taking it back to the dealer and complaining that we had checked our oils and fluids and tires religiously, so why was this happening, and the dealer kept saying, "Ladies, your car is eleven years old. You got a hundred and sixty-two thousand miles on it. What that is, is fantastic. Super. Terrific. I don't think you have any complaints coming. What you need to do is, you need to buy a new one. We got a fabulous new model that —" — that cost about ten times what we could possibly afford.

For two weeks we tried living without a car. Mother could take a bus to work if she walked five blocks to catch it and nine blocks from there to the office. Grocery shopping is not fun when you're a half mile from the store. We did that twice without a car and twice with a taxi and each time the ice cream melted. Going to the library required a car. Going to the doctor or school games or the shopping malls required a car.

We were, however, getting enough exercise that Mother never wanted to run up and down the stairs fifteen times to limber up.

Then one day she could not pick up a client, I could not get home from a club meeting, and neither of us had taxi fare. That was the day we realized we were going to have to get another car. "Five hundred for your old one," said the dealer, as if he were being incredibly generous. Maybe he was.

Which meant, even buying a completely stripped-down model, we needed several thousand more dollars.

"I guess," said my mother, almost crying, "it's time we found out if kitchen antiques are really an investment." For another few days she walked around the apartment stroking her jars, bowls, choppers, spoons, toddy sticks, graters (carefully), butter molds, and candle boxes. I went baby-sitting and earned six dollars. Some spectacular contribution. I job-hunted. Fast food places had waiting lists. Department stores had hired all the temporary help they needed. Factories were laying off, not extending. Offices only wanted people who typed.

Mother went to a bank to see about a car loan and found that since she had last borrowed for that purpose interest rates had gotten very high. The car would cost so much that the car loan would actually be higher than our rent. There was no way we could afford payments.

"Okay," said Mother. "Time to start pricing this stuff. It's got to go. All of it."

"But Mother, you've spent years collecting this. Just sell some of it, Mother. If you sell it all you'll be depressed. We'd just end up buying it back on our weekend hunts."

"No. We're not doing that anymore. I've thrown away far too much money and time on that silly hobby." She stroked a cherry dough trough that still had its milk-base paint on two sides. "We need to start thinking about how on earth you're going to get through college."

"Mother, we decided years ago I'd go to college right here and live at home and go on loans for tuition if I can't get scholarships."

"Just my Coca Cola collection could probably pay for your first year," she said. She knelt over a dusty cache of Coca Cola memorabilia — bottles, caps, trays, clocks, ads, carriers, and so forth — that filled up the corner under the hanging antique baskets.

There was truthfully not one object of Mother's that I would miss. The clutter exasperates me. Sometimes I fantasize about having an apartment of my own. It'll have wall-to-wall carpet, either deep rust or bright navy blue; sometimes I change my mind and visualize beige. Cream-colored walls to show off artwork. One single clock — long, thin, and modern. Tailored custom Roman shades at the windows. No clutter. No dust. No mess. No collections of anything except friends.

Mother sat at the kitchen table (all our tables are kitchen tables; we've got about six kitchen tables) and began composing the advertisements she'd need to put in dozens of newspapers. She wasn't crying, but she looked sort of beaten.

It was so unfair. Mother worked hard and sometimes she was lonely, and this hobby was really a major part of her life. How awful to have to dispose of it in order to have four wheels.

"Perhaps," said Mother thoughtfully, "perhaps I'll call David and Catherine Nearing and ask their advice. One of them might be willing to come up and help me run the sale. They've been in the business for thirty years. And if they're not my cousins, they ought to be."

"They'd be Father's cousins," I said.

"I've been a Nearing half my life. Let's see if blood runs thicker than water." She reached for the telephone.

"Mother, how can you ask such a big favor of somebody you've only met once? What if he can't remember you? We already owe him a lot for all that time and dinner and everything. What if he doesn't want to do it except for a fee?" I felt embarrassed just thinking about the phone call.

"I wouldn't ask him to do it without a fee," said Mother. "Stop worrying. The worst that could happen is that either David or Catherine will say no."

I actually had to leave the room when she was calling. Sometimes I have to do that during television comedies when you know the girl is going to be in a perfectly humiliating situation and do something stupid and get laughed at. I can't stand it. I have to walk away and come back during the ads.

Then I thought: What if Mr. Nearing brings Nicholas with him?

I ran back to listen to the phone call.

Mother was laughing and nodding into the phone. Lots of unrevealing umhmms, and yes indeeds, and for heaven's sakeses. "Wonderful," she said at last, and gave him street directions to our apartment.

"What's happening?" I demanded.

"David is coming. He's going to an antique show in Richmond to exhibit and he's going to leave one day earlier and come by. We'll take a look at what I have and talk about how to handle the sale. Oh, Nannie, I'm so glad I called him. Sometimes it's a lot easier to go ahead with something when you have someone else agreeing that it's intelligent. It'll be so much easier to price things, for example. And decide what to list in the ads."

"Is he bringing Aunt Catherine or Nick along?" I said casually.

"Catherine can't get away for three whole days. Isn't that a shame?"

"Yes, it is." I waited. Mother didn't say anything more. At last I had to say, "And what about Nick? Is he coming?"

"Oh yes. David says he always forces Nick to come to help man the booth. Nick hates it. David is dreading the day Nick leaves for college because he doesn't think Nick will ever come back."

I was grinning from ear to ear. "Oh yes, he'll come back," I said. I felt carbonated: My heart was tickling.

"How do you know?" said Mother.

"He told me." I went to my room and shut the door so I could think about Nick.

In honor of their visit, we cooked everything from the Daughters of the Confederacy Cookbook. We had N. C. Nearing's corn gems (which were just molasses-flavored corn muffins), Miss Mary Metcalfe Nearing's chicken and onions, Mrs. Anne Kingsley's stewed collards, and Miss Nelle Nearing's fried apple pies.

We had a terrible time with the pies. Nelle of course knew just how to do it, but she assumed that you did too and only gave you the ingredients. "Add flour till dough is ready," she wrote —only neither Mother nor I knew when we were ready. Nor did old Nelle tell how long to fry the pies. We found the answer to that in a *New York Times Cookbook* a neighbor had. We finally got them done, but they were so fragile that if you picked one up carelessly, you got a lap full of apple filling.

"Gosh, they're good, though, aren't they?" said Mother, wolfing one down.

I ate one too. It *was* terrific. We could hardly manage to keep our fingers off them so as to leave enough for Nick and his father.

I was extremely nervous.

Oddly enough, what worried me most was that Nick would not be as wonderful as I remembered him. Perhaps I had made him all up, and he was really just a boring ordinary boy. We might not know what to do with a long blank evening ahead of us.

"Hi, Nancy," he said, strolling in as if he'd visited this set of cousins dozens of times.

"How've you been? You're right, it's a rotten drive up here. No direct route at all. I don't know how you did it, after midnight, being so tired. What smells so good?"

"Fried pies."

"I thought you hated to cook."

"I do, but it was fun cooking for somebody that . . ." I almost said, "somebody that I really care about," but I stopped in time and said, ". . . that I feel like feeding well."

Nick deftly palmed one of the little half-moon shaped pies. He had obviously eaten them before and knew enough to hold it carefully. He'd eaten the whole thing before Mother could tell him not to eat his dessert first. "That's as good as Aunt Catherine's," he said. "She doesn't make them much anymore. Too hard."

But Mother wasn't watching Nick eat his dessert first. She was taking Mr. Nearing around the apartment and he was exclaiming appropriately over this and that, uttering little cries of delight and thin whistles of appreciation. Nick said, "Is it like this all the time around here?"

"Antiques, you mean? Yes. Wall to wall."

"When I have an apartment of my own, it's going to be streamlined. No nothing in there but me and my clothes and maybe a chair and a television."

"Sounds like the one I'm going to have. Although I'll add a chair for guests and a bookcase."

"Nope, you don't want shelves." Nick shook his head vigorously and his ponytail bounced. "You get shelves, next thing you know you'll be wanting things to put on them. Before long you'll need more shelves, and maybe even a drawer or two. Next thing you know, you'll have to move to a bigger place to hold all your junk. No, Nancy, you do not want shelves."

"I need a place for books."

"Use the library."

"You're even worse than I am," I said. "How can you possibly convince any of your father's customers to buy anything when you hate everything he's selling?"

"Are you kidding? I *love* selling the stuff. Then there's less of it."

We burst out laughing. Nick ate another fried pie. "Have one," he said, "they're good." So I had one.

His father took out a stenography notebook and busily wrote down descriptions while he and Mother haggled about prices as if one of them actually intended to buy. "All right, all right," he said, "if you really think so. I still believe you could get eighty for that. Now this one over here is in mint condition."

I heated up the dinner and served it. Conversation was erratic, to say the least.

"Did you ever locate my father in your genealogy tables?" I asked Mr. Nearing.

"No, Nancy, I never did. Now, Eleanor," he said to my mother, "I think we've got to decide if you'd do better selling the butter molds as a group or singly."

"Have another corn gem," said Nick to me, as if he had made them.

"Frankly, this is such a good collection I think we should call up one of these high-powered New York dealers and see if somebody would like to buy the whole thing. In case we get some interest from that angle, we need to have a complete price in mind," said Nick's father.

"I think these have too much molasses," said my mother.

"What molasses?" said Mr. Nearing, looking around — for antique molasses, I suppose.

"The corn gems," said my mother. "Now, David, I have to keep some things. I'll be desolate if we clear it out completely."

"Well, stack the things you'll be keeping in Nancy's room."

"*My* room!" I yelped.

"It's the only one without antiques. That way we won't get mixed up." He buttered another corn gem. Nick ate the last fried pie.

"Except I don't know what to keep," she said. "I love everything."

"So much for streamlined, shelfless privacy," said Nick, grinning.

"It's a common problem for antique dealers," said his father to my mother. "Logically you should sell what's worth the most and keep the junk, but of course what you want to keep are the real goodies."

"I bought them for a rainy day," said my mother, "and it's definitely raining." She didn't sound glum, though, but as if she were having fun. Making a party out of selling her treasures had definitely been the right idea for her.

"Nancy?" said Nick. "Since I have to live and breathe antiques at the Richmond show for two solid days, I'd love to escape them tonight."

"Sounds good to me. What would you like to do?"

Nick looked suddenly awkward and uncomfortable. I didn't know what to make of it — unless he felt like escaping from me, too, and I had misinterpreted his remark. He said, "Well, I'm kind of broke, actually. So something like a movie would be, well — "

"You can't be as broke as I am," I said. "I can't even get an ice cream cup at school anymore. Otherwise I'd treat you."

"What kind of neighborhood is this? Walking type? After dark?"

It was definitely a walking-after-dark type neighborhood. Nick didn't know it, but sauntering slowly, hand in hand with a special boy, in my own neighborhood, as the sun set, was a particular little tiny fantasy of mine. Holly says I have crummy fantasies: I should at least daydream about walking over the moors of Scotland, or something.

"You shouldn't spend all this money on a brand-new car," said Mr. Nearing. "Get a good buy in a used one and get a station wagon or a van this time. You need hauling room. Say, Eleanor, I love this cupboard. Flour sifter, knife holder, and meat grinder original and intact. Gosh. Wouldn't you like to build a house just for your stuff, Eleanor? You know, with a huge old-fashioned kitchen for all your tables and cupboards and stoves and irons?"

Shuddering simultaneously, Nick and I left. "Look on the bright side," said Nick. "By the time one of them figures out where to get the money to build such a house, we'll be safely off at college."

We walked six blocks to the city lake and sat

down on a bench. The sun was setting in front of us and we stared into threads of gold and pink and silver. A jet trail whipped a diagonal line through the sunset.

It's funny. Whenever I daydream about a date with a boy (not Nick) I always have us *doing* something. Going to the ice cream store, seeing a movie, driving the car, hitting the tennis ball, riding horses. I never include *talking* in the daydream, mostly because I can never imagine myself succeeding in this. What did one say to a boy, a breed I was the first to admit I did not understand?

But now, with this boy — we were doing nothing *but* talking, and it was wonderful. We traded stories and ideas and thoughts as easily as we had the other time.

Nick stretched out, half off the bench, balancing on the back of his neck and the base of his spine. It looked very uncomfortable to me but Nick claimed to be relaxed. Whatever else it was, it wasn't a position to kiss in.

Still, I could study his face and think about kissing it.

And then the turkey repeated the only line from our first evening that I hadn't liked. "Always nice to be talking to a cousin," he said, yawning, as if I were blending in very nicely with the rest of that crowd. "I always find a cousin easier to talk to than a regular girl, know what I mean?"

Eight

"Ann Landers had a column about that," said Ginger. "You can marry your cousin unless he's a first cousin, and in some states you can even do that."

"Ginger, will you get off this marriage thing? I just want a boyfriend."

"Take mine, I'm done with him."

"Listen, you couldn't *sell* Keith," said Holly. "You couldn't even give Keith away."

"He wasn't that bad. I got out, at least."

We had to admit that going out was more than Holly and I had achieved.

"When is the big kitchen sale coming up?" said Holly.

"I'm not sure we're having one after all. Nick's father called up a few dealers in New York he knows and one of the big department stores is having a kitchenwares display and they want to take a look at Mother's entire collection — to use as background."

"You mean all her pretty things would be somebody's purple plastic stacking mug set's scenery?" said Ginger. "Tacky, very tacky."

"Ginger, you're the only person I know who talks like a tongue twister," said Holly. "Are either of you going to the Final Fling?"

The Final Fling is a big dance open to all three grades of the high school, held the second-to-last weekend of the school year. It's casual, with people mostly wearing jeans and sneakers. There are a lot of prizes for each dance, which are more elimination contests than dances. Last year I went with Peter Franciola but he only asked me because he wanted to go to the Final Fling and not because he liked me very much. I wouldn't even classify it as a date, because we hardly even talked to each other, although he did bring me a glass of punch.

Holly was going this year with Chuck Summers. She didn't even like him. The only thing worse than not going would be going with someone you don't want to spend ten minutes with, let alone an evening of public dancing. Ginger, it turned out, was actually going with a cousin, having broken up with Keith.

"You should have timed your break-up better," Holly told her.

"My cousin's all right. He's safe, if you know what I mean. I won't get embarrassed," said Ginger. "Why don't you ask Nick, Nancy? We could double. Double cousins."

Since I had the perfect excuse for not calling him I handled that one easily. "If he lived next door I would," I said, "but I can't ask him to drive one hundred seventy miles just for a dumb dance."

"You are overly fixated on that one hundred seventy miles," said Ginger.

"Try driving it. You'd think it was quite an obstacle, too."

"I keep thinking of that phrase 'regular girl,'" said Holly. "I guess Nick feels the same way Ginger does about her cousin. Safe."

"Correct," said Ginger. "Nicholas was saying he, too, is awkward on formal dates and in conversations with girls with whom he is supposed to be forming romantic relationships, whereas cousins preclude such nervousness."

"That was very good, Ginger," I said. "You get one hundred in vocabulary."

"Would you like me to reiterate my statements? I could embellish on that theme."

We declined Ginger's offer and parted company to go to our classes. And there I was, two weeks before the end of school, and Holly and Ginger were going to the Final Fling and I was not.

I had sort of thought that getting practice talking with Nick would show on me. As if the boys passing in the corridor would now take a second look at Nancy Nearing and see right off that this girl would be easy and funny to talk to. A real joy to be around. The perfect date.

No such luck.

"Nancy, the man from Bloomingdale's was here," said Mother.

"Bloomingdale's?"

"In New York, silly. The department store. Actually there were three of them. One man who was very slim and elegant and two women who were terribly slender and fashionable. I felt like a blimp."

"I know the feeling."

"Anyway, they offered a package price for everything I have — from the three quilts right down to the lemon squeezers — that was two thousand dollars more than the maximum David and I had figured on!"

"Oh, Mother. How fantastic!"

"You haven't heard anything yet. I sort of stood there, completely stunned, and tried to take it in. My head was just spinning with thoughts of all that money, and darn if they didn't up their offer another thousand."

"Wow. You should have gone right on standing there."

"I tried it for a while, but they seemed to revise their opinion of me. No longer a shrewd businesswoman, just a retarded housewife."

We giggled and patted each other.

"They'll be here in a van tomorrow," she said, "and I sold everything."

"Mother! Everything?"

"Everything. They went into your room and of course they loved all that stuff too, and in the end I agreed to sell every single antique we had."

I opened my bedroom door. Selling what lay on my bed and filled my floors would be like selling her children. When I turned around again my mother was sitting on the couch, weeping. "Oh, Nancy," she said, "it's so *stupid* to care about things like cheese graters. Imagine crying over them! But I can't help it. Oh, honey, I hope the money is worth it."

In the morning's mail was a letter from Nick. I had never mailed my own note to Nick. I had never gotten past the first line. I held the letter and tried to think when I had ever gotten any personal mail.

I had actually hugged the envelope to my chest when something struck me. It was Nick's name on the return address — but it was my *mother's* name on the mailing address!

I almost tore up the envelope! Writing to my mother — how could he! A thank you note, obviously. How courteous and proper of him.

The turkey.

I gave the letter to Mother and had to restrain myself from stomping all the way into my bedroom. I wanted to slam the door so much that I had to tuck it gently into its grooves.

Mother barely glanced at it. The moving men had arrived and were packing her antiques as if they were going on exhibit beside a Michaelangelo sculpture — piles of excelsior and peanut-shaped styrofoam filled every box.

It was like watching an orange being peeled. Bit by bit the living room was no longer hers, no longer the lifelong collection she'd built. It became a naked, stark place with just a few old rugs and a sagging sofa and an old television. In fact, the room that emerged from beneath the clutter of Mother's treasures was — there's no nice way to put it — a dump.

For some time Mother's face crumpled, like the packing paper the moving men were so carefully using. She was watching her antiques leaving as if it were her children being sold.

"What did Nick want, Mother?" I said.

"Oh, he's got some college interview scheduled in the area. He wants to spend the night here or something. Call him up and tell him it's okay, Nannie. If he doesn't mind lumps, he can have the couch. Or he could bring a sleeping bag. I don't know but the floor might be better than that couch."

Planning a phone conversation as important as that would take time and privacy. I made myself a cup of tea (I always think better with my hands wrapped around something hot — it's almost as good as a hot shower for meditating) and walked slowly, not letting it spill over, into my bedroom.

There were two moving men in there. "Hey!" I cried. "You're not supposed to pack those! Those are my stuffed animals and my bed pillows! Bloomingdale's only bought the antiques."

"Sorry, lady," said one of them, "they looked old to me."

I don't know which was the odder idea, that my Barbie doll sets belonged in the kitchen antique collection or that this guy should say to me "Sorry, lady." I got no privacy, though. I had to spend the afternoon supervising, because they wanted to pack my torn gothic paperbacks and my set of heart-shaped throw pillows and the empty perfume bottles lining the window sill.

When they finally left, Mother and I sat down in the living room, almost panting with relief. It was horribly empty. Large dust kittens and spiderwebs were revealed where piles of old spice containers and hat boxes had stood. The ceiling hooks where the basket collection had been hanging were silly metal dabs on a fingerprinted ceiling. The tear in the carpet that had been covered by the thread chest and the old cash register was exposed again, and on the wall where the sunburst quilt had hung was a dusty depressing rectangle.

In the entire apartment, there was no color, no texture, nothing pretty, and nothing interesting.

We sat listening to the refrigerator hum, and Mother looked at the check they'd given her and told me about eleven times that it was worth it, yes, Nannie, it was definitely worth it. And then she burst into tears.

"Oh, Mom, it'll be all right," I said desperately. "We can get more. That's enough money for a car and some college savings and lots left over to redecorate. It'll be pretty again, you'll see." I perched on the sofa back and tried patting Mother's shoulder.

"Oh, honey, it's so awful to see this place without my things. I could pretend it was a home before. Now it's just a nasty cheap little apartment."

I sat beside her, and she was right, the couch was awfully lumpy. I tried to hug her, but it's hard to comfort your own mother.

"Oh God, Nancy," she said, wiping at her tears with the back of her hand. "In another two years you'll be leaving, and I won't even have any of the things I've built my life around. This is so stupid, this is so colossally *stupid*, weeping like this for cheese graters, for heaven's sake." She tried to laugh, but it wasn't very successful.

"It's okay to love things, Mom. It isn't stupid."

She stopped crying and looked at me with an expression that was almost dislike. It scared me. "You never thought so before, Nancy. I'm surprised you're not rejoicing. Having a party. Calling all your friends over to see the nice bare modern apartment, the one you've always dreamed about."

"Mother! That's not what I meant."

"Oh, really? You've been talking about your wall-to-wall carpet and your chrome etagères ever since I can remember. You were actually in there helping those moving men."

"Mother, I was just making sure they didn't take any of my things."

"Exactly. They can take everything *I* have, but nothing of yours!"

"But, Mother, Bloomingdale's didn't buy any of *my* things! What would they want with secondhand Harlequin romances? And it was your idea to sell it all, not mine. I said to keep at least a few things for yourself."

"You need the money for college," she said, "and we couldn't manage without a car. There was no choice. I hate it when there aren't any choices. I hate all these women's magazine articles about everything being okay if you just have faith in yourself. *I hate this apartment!*"

I felt as if some stranger was yelling at me. My mother, who was always sweet and understanding and willing, unable to control her feelings. All the raw edges were exposed in front of me.

She kept saying that it wasn't a *home* anymore, it was just an apartment.

"You want me to call the state police and have them stop the van?" I said, only half joking. "We could return the check and pay the movers ourselves for their time."

"With what money? The only money we have *is* this check." Mother walked into her bedroom and shut the door in my face. I had done that to her many times, but she had never done it to me. I knew how she felt, needing that door between her and everything else, needing to be shut in privately to think. But it hurt terribly to watch that door close and know she just did not want me near her.

Nine

"Nick," I said, using my sexiest voice (or at least, the one I think is sexiest — never having had a reaction to any of my vocal selections, I don't really know), "this is Nancy Nearing. The one from Virginia, remember?"

No, no good. I didn't like that choice. I sounded as if I didn't expect anybody to remember me, faceless personality that I was. I rehearsed it another way. "Hello there, Nick! It's Nancy!"

And what if he really wasn't sure which N.C. Nearing I was?

Maybe I should skip the name. "Hi, Nick. Mother says to tell you we'd be glad to have you spend the night."

Actually, she wasn't glad at all. She was ashamed of the apartment. We'd cleaned it ferociously, and somehow that made the place worse. Now it was scrubbed emptiness and there was no trace of it ever having any character or hominess. Mother didn't feel like having visitors.

When I finally did manage to get my fingers up to the telephone dial and make the call, I got Aunt Catherine. "Nancy Nearing?" she said, puzzled. "It doesn't sound like you, honey, we must have a bad connection. How's Everett doing? He over his strep throat yet?"

"I think that's a different Nancy Nearing," I said. "I'm the one who drove in from Virginia and we tried to figure out if we were related?"

"Oh yes. That's right. And are you?"

"Excuse me? Am I what?"

"Related."

"Oh. I don't think we ever found out."

"Uh huh. Well. Were you calling about antiques, then?"

"No, ma'am. I wanted to speak to Nick."

"Nick?" she said, as if she had never heard of him. I began to wonder if I myself had the right Nearing in mind. In great embarrassment I said, "Nick Nearing? With the ponytail?"

"Oh." She laughed heartily. I held the phone away from my ear and my stomach knotted up again. I hate phone calls that don't work according to my rehearsals. "You mean Ency," she said. "Yes, of course, he's right here."

I had this terrible fear that "Ency" would be somebody else entirely. I would have this long conversation with some girl, also named N. C. Nearing, who happened to have long red hair in a ponytail. Nick was a mirage and his letter a dream.

"Hello, Nancy," said Nick. "Sorry about that. Aunt Catherine gets very confused sometimes. Thanks for calling back."

I sagged with relief. "We're looking forward to having you," I said.

"Oh, terrific. You sure I won't be a nuisance to your mother?"

Maybe he knew he'd be no nuisance to me. "No problem," I said, although in fact, Mother was uptight at the idea of an overnight guest on her dreadfully lumpy couch. "You might want to bring a sleeping bag, though. We haven't got a guest bed."

"I could sleep on the couch, couldn't I?"

"Sure, if you like lumps."

"I like lumps better than floors. I've got an interview that Friday afternoon in Richmond so I'll get to your place about supper time. And Saturday morning I've got two more scheduled, one at ten and one at eleven-thirty. Your place is really convenient and I really appreciate your mother saying I can stay."

Your mother, your mother. Why did he have to keep dragging my mother into this? At least he wasn't using his retread voice.

He sounded like another person altogether. Brisk and efficient. I'd met the funny Nick, the tape-recorded Nick, and now here was another Nick. Brisk and efficient. No doubt a fine way to approach things. I reminded myself that anything Ginger could do, I could do. I told myself that cousins were easier to talk to than regular people. I said — out loud, without rehearsal or planning or dreaming — "As a matter of fact, there's a dance at my school that night. Would you like to go with me?"

He did not answer.

My stomach twinged instantly. "Never mind,"

I said hastily. "I'm sure you'll be tired after all that driving and interviewing and all."

"No, I'm just trying to think about clothes. I wasn't going to bring anything for, you know, for a dance. I'm not sure I even own anything. I—"

"No, no, no, no. That's no problem. It's a jeans-and-shirt dance. I'm wearing my old faded Wranglers and a pink ruffled blouse and—" I broke off. As if Nicholas Nearing cared whether my blouse had pink ruffles.

"Well, okay. If you want," he said, noticeably lacking enthusiasm. I remembered that Nick was the sort of courteous person who opened doors and wrote thank you letters. No doubt he also went to dances when his hostess placed the demand upon him.

"Well, I don't want to drag you to it," I said, trying to sound highly amused by his reluctance.

"No, no, it's okay. Great. I'm looking forward to it."

Tape-recorded, definitely a retread remark. I said helplessly, "Fine. I'll see you Friday."

"I'll bring my jeans."

"Great."

"Yeah. Bye."

I hung up and said "Yuck" to my Barbie doll collection. I'd done it. I'd asked the boy to the dance. And he'd said yes. It wasn't much of a yes, it was a very dutiful yes, but still it was a yes. And with my scintillating personality, no doubt I could manage to turn Friday into an evening so wonderful Nick would never forget it.

"Believe it," I said sarcastically to my Barbies. Barbie never gets turned down when she wants

Ken to go to a dance. Ken has never done anything but grin in his entire life.

I sat awake that night making mental lists of interesting topics that Nick and I could talk about.

Next day I spent study hour in the guidance office reading up on the three colleges where Nick was having his interviews. They were good schools. I wondered what kind of grades and college boards Nick had. What he wanted to major in. What his interests and hobbies were. All I knew about Nick's future was that he planned not to have it unfold in Nearing River.

In a way it was good to be so totally ignorant about Nick. How could we possibly run out of conversation when we had his entire life to discuss?

I went to history smiling to myself, and turning to the next blank page of my notebook I wrote "Nicholas" in medieval letters. After class Rod Holmes stopped me in the hall and asked me to go with him to the Final Fling.

For a moment I just stared at him.

I liked Rod. A lot. I always had. Now that I'd made one phone call to a boy and lived through the ordeal of one invitation to a dance, I had a glimmer of an idea of what it felt like to nerve oneself to extend invitations. To get oneself ready to catch a girl by the sleeve and say, Hey, Nance, wait a sec, listen, say, you want to go with me . . .

I hated turning him down. I hated it because of the way my stomach and head had felt when Nick had answered me so slowly and reluctantly.

I didn't want to do that to anybody else. "Oh, Rod, I'd love to," I said. His face lit up and I felt like a sap. "I wish you'd asked me yesterday." And I did wish it. What could be worse than going to the Final Fling with a guy who went because your mother was letting him stay at your place and he had to be polite about it? "But I'm going with — well, actually, my cousin is in town and I asked him to take me."

If anything Rod looked glad to hear this. All my sympathetic feelings evaporated and I was just infuriated. How dare he be *glad* I couldn't go?

"Gee, that's too bad," he said happily. "Well, maybe I'll see you there. I might go stag."

We stared at each other. Really, boys are mysterious.

"But how about a Coke this afternoon?" said Rod, still happy with how things were turning out. "Are you busy or could we go to Hardee's or someplace and have a Coke?"

I was busy. I had a meeting for next year's yearbook committee. I began to understand why attendance at this sort of meeting was erratic. Choices have to be made and I know where my duty lies. But I also know no boy has ever asked me out before, and besides, I didn't want to see Rod smile even *wider* if I said no. "I'd love to. I'll meet you by the band room after seventh period, okay?"

"Good enough," and Rod was gone, galloping down the hall and vanishing into the stairwell.

We had to go past the elementary school on our way to Hardee's. A bunch of little kids were playing out among the swing sets. "I used to love doing that," said Rod.

"Doing what?" I said. There were two little boys pouncing on the tiny girls who foolishly walked past the hemlock hedge. Was that what he used to love doing? I watched the girls scream and aim strong kicks at the boys, who leaped backwards. Ah, to be six years old and know which team you're on.

"Jungle gyms," he said. "Slides, too. And sandboxes, of course. I was crazy about swings. I remember thinking I was so tough the first time I hung by my knees from the top of the jungle gym."

I'd worn trousers that day instead of the lavender skirt my mother had suggested at breakfast. I knew I had good instincts; I congratulated myself. "Bet I can climb it faster than you can, Rod." I raced over the hopscotch pavement and across the grass to the jungle gym. Rod passed me like a horse going for the Derby and shot up the jungle gym before I had even arrived.

We hung companionably upside down for a while.

I watched Rod's face get redder and redder. "I'd forgotten about growing," said Rod sadly, his hair brushing in the sand.

"It's supposed to be for six-year-olds, not six-footers," I agreed. My hair and I were short enough not to touch the ground. I wondered if Nick would have done this with me. What would Rod think of Nick and his ponytail? Would he notice it, or care? Rod gave my rear end a push and swung me. The little kids came over to watch and we stared back at them from upside down.

"You look dumb," said a little girl solemnly.

"Yeah, but we feel great," said Rod. He swung up, straddled the pole, yelled horsey sounds, and pretended to ride his steed away from the bad guys. The little kids were really impressed by that and immediately mounted poles of their own. We all jumped fences and leaped chasms until I lost my balance whinnying too loud and tumbled off. Rod scraped me out of the sand, brushing it off my clothes, paying a lot more attention to this than I would have. The little kids, who were small but not dumb, made many remarks about it.

"So much for our second childhoods," said Rod. "Let us proceed."

For some reason we hobbled along, as if our legs were tied together for a three-legged race. Clinging to each other, we staggered and giggled, Rod yelling things like, "Almost there! And the finish line is in sight! Come on, team!"

The instant we reached the sidewalk, we moved apart and continued very sedately on our way. Rod began to speak with an English accent and I stopped speaking altogether and just laughed.

At Hardee's we took a booth for two near the window so we could, as Rod said, have an unblocked view of the parking lot and the gas station. We sipped our Cokes. Actually mine was Mello Yello and Rod's was Dr. Pepper, but still, it was a sort of a Coke date. "Rod?" I said, feeling brave.

"Yeah?"

"How come you were, well, sort of glad when I couldn't come to the Final Fling with you?"

"Oh, you mean you could tell?"

"It was the wide grin that gave you away."

"I'm sorry, I really am. I . . . well, the truth is, my mother made me promise her I'd ask somebody to the dance. But I hate the thought of even trying to dance. The night of the Final Fling I plan to be rebuilding the brakes on my car."

I laughed so hard the Mello Yello dribbled out of my mouth and I had to wipe myself up with a napkin. "Then why'd you ask me for Cokes?" I said. "Your mother insist on that, too?"

"Aw, don't hold that against me." Rod made a helpless face. I grinned at him and he smiled back. His teeth were crooked, but not enough for braces, just enough to be sort of attractive. "I drink Cokes fine," he said. "It's one of my better skills. It's just dancing I don't do.

"I see. You were so grateful to me for *not* going to the dance with you, you wanted to reward me."

"Aw, stop teasing me. I just wanted to have a date, okay? Without dancing."

We kidded around until the manager began to send us meaningful glances. They have a new rule in all the hamburger places near the high school: No teenagers can stay more than half an hour. The kids were cluttering up the restaurants so much that adults wouldn't come in anymore. I can see the managers' point, but when you're making friends or on your first real date, half an hour is not long enough. "Actually," I said, "I'm supposed to be at that yearbook meeting. I'd better run back."

"I heard that announced, Nancy, it started right after school!" Rod sounded concerned.

"Yes, it did, but I wanted to . . . well, you know, have a Coke." That sounded so stupid. I tried to say that I'd wanted to accept, and be with him, but I couldn't get the words out. Rod apparently didn't mind, or he understood without my having to say so. He walked me — swiftly — back to school and we agreed we'd have to do it again sometime.

So I went into the meeting, which was wrapping up, feeling guilty for purposely missing it, and feeling absolutely wonderful that Rod wanted my company.

"Nancy," said the editor, "while you were gone, you were elected chairman of advertising sales."

"Oh no!" I yelped. "I resign. I refuse. I wanted to do favorite quotes."

"Favorite quotes went to Jeannine. Those who are not present to decline nomination cannot argue with the decision of the majority." The editor smiled wickedly. She was right, I'd skipped out. I gave up and agreed to be in charge of advertising. Already my next school year was looking grim.

Except, of course, for Rod. And Nick. The maybe of my love life.

Ten

"Nick?" I said. *"Nick?"*

He was as embarrassed as a sixth-grader the first day out in public in his braces. He flushed, looking like he didn't want to come in. The fact that I was standing in the doorway may have contributed to this difficulty. "Hi," he mumbled.

I couldn't help myself. I reached out and ran my fingers over the back of his head where his ponytail had been. "I love it," I said, shaking my head in surprise. "But I thought you weren't going to cut it off for another year. You know. Matter of principle and demanding relatives and kidding friends and all that."

He shrugged and tugged at his clothes, now that he could not tug at his hair. "I panicked about my college interviews. I had on this three-piece suit and I was buttoning up the vest and in the mirror I noticed this ponytail bouncing around between my shoulder blades. With this stupid red rubber band around it. All of a sudden I knew I couldn't get through an interview with a ponytail. So I cut it off."

"Well, it looks terrific. I love it."

"Really? You do?" He looked as if he really cared about my opinion. My heart lifted about a yard. I felt out of breath, as if an elevator had whisked me up there with my heart. "Yes, I do," I said.

Nick nodded about twenty times over that. "Besides," he said, "you asked me to this dance of yours. Now, in Nearing River, everybody knows me. They're used to my hair. They expect my hair. In fact, they're going to laugh at me without my hair. But at your high school, I'd have to get introduced to all these strangers and there'd be this ponytail in the way, and all their eyebrows going up, looking at me. You know?"

I burst out laughing. "And to think when I first met you at Nearing River House, I thought you were completely cool and relaxed."

"I am at ease there. It gives me the Continental soldier look. Or it did. I don't know how I'll look now." He explored the short hair with a nervous hand. "Look, Nancy, can I come in or am I going to be sleeping out here in the stairwell?"

I jumped out of the doorway. "No, of course not. I mean, yes, come in. I'm sorry. I forgot about you. I mean, I didn't forget, I —"

Nick put his index finger over my lips to stop my babbling and walked in. I looked at his passing profile and then his back and I thought, Is he ever cute!

"Nick!" exclaimed my mother. "Good heavens. I wouldn't have known you. Glen plaid suit with vest and leather belt. Neatly cut hair. Polished shoes. You look so respectable."

"Mother," I said irritably, "he looked perfectly respectable before."

"No, he looked interesting before. Not respectable. I like it, Nick. It's an immense improvement."

"That," said Nick, groaning, "is a taste of what I'll have to go through when I get back to Nearing River. How much I've improved. Which means, of course, that I was never up to snuff before."

"Up to snuff," said mother. "My goodness, what an antique expression. You'll have to be careful, Nick, your father's profession is infecting you."

"You mean," I asked him, "that nobody has seen your short hair yet?"

"It isn't short, Nancy," said my mother. "It's a lot less long, but it isn't short." It was clear that she felt a second visit to the barber was in order and the sooner the better. Nick cast his eyes ceilingward. "No," he said, "I cut it in Richmond, just about an hour before my interview. Even my father and my Aunt Catherine don't know."

"They'll be so pleased," said my mother, patting him. "Really, Nick, it's such a sign of your growing up. You look adult for a change."

Nick made a face.

"I see what you mean," I said to him. "It's going to be awful, isn't it?"

"I figure I've got a three-day weekend in Virginia to get used to myself and kind of prepare to face the music," said Nick. He sank onto the couch and began frowning. I thought the frown was for all nagging relatives back in Nearing River until I saw his eyes going from corner to corner, examining our apartment. "Well," he said, "the place is . . . well . . . it's . . . it's —"

"Horrible," said my mother.

I was trying to think of something cheering to say to her when Nick said fervently, "It sure is. I never thought anything would make me want to get back to antiques. What are you going to do to fix it up?"

I was completely astonished when Mother leaned forward as if to tell Nick a confidence. "I thought I'd start with new paint," she said. "I'm sick of these cream-colored walls. Especially where you can see the lighter places where my quilts hung. What would you think of shiny cranberry red for the window wall and a slick royal blue for the rest of the room? Maybe lemon yellow mini-blinds for the windows and emerald green upholstery for the chairs?"

We gaped at her. "That doesn't sound very early American," said Nick in the sort of voice his Aunt Catherine would use if she couldn't understand you.

"I've been through my early American stage," said Mother firmly. "I'm reaching out for something else. I've always liked bright colors. I want a whole rainbow in here. Something that will smack you in the face when you open the door."

"It'll be cheerful," said Nick doubtfully.

"What about beige?" I said.

"Beige! I've had it with the natural look. All those tans and neutrals and wood and weeds. They sent me photographs from Bloomingdale's showing their kitchen exhibit and you should see some of that stuff. They've built all sorts of levels and cabinetry and barn-siding walls and rippling kitcheny areas, with my old things sort of hanging around for atmosphere against all the walls — but up front! You should see up front! Purple laminated Parsons tables and brushed stainless steel lamps and lucite napkin rings and —"

"Good grief," said Nick. "Talk about turning over a new leaf. And all I did was cut my hair."

We all three began laughing helplessly, looking at the disaster that was the living room and imagining Mother's lemon yellow blinds, scarlet walls, and brushed stainless steel lamps.

"How about supper?" said Nick. "As long as you'll settle for cheeseburgers and french fries, it's my treat."

"I," said Mother brightly, "have this marvelous idea."

We looked at her nervously.

"No, no, not decorating the apartment. My idea is, since I want to lose some weight and I do not need french fries nor burger buns, you two go by yourselves and live it up. Have dessert. Go all out. I'll stay here and have a cup of bouillon and meditate on whether I want lime green or pumpkin orange mugs."

"You sure?" said Nick. "A cup of bouillon sounds depressing."

"It is. Anything slimming is depressing."

"Come with us," said Nick again, and he really seemed worried. Did he really not want Mother to have bouillon, or did he not want to be alone with me? I had a piercing thought that as long as Mother was along, we were cousins — but alone, we might be a date. And all Nick wanted, as he'd so clearly told me, was to get away from the long endless cluttered line of N. C. Nearings. I shook off the thought. "Well, Nick," I said, "let's go then. See you after the dance, Mother."

Nick clattered down the three flights of stairs without waiting for me. His knees kind of poked out to the sides when he moved, while mine went straight out frontwards. I loved watching him. He was moving like blue jeans, but he was wearing a suit.

It was funny. For years and years, all through elementary school, I had no use for boys. They were wild noisy animals with claws for fingernails and burps for conversation.

I can distinctly remember sitting in seventh-grade science, pretending to care about stamens and pistils when an eighth-grade boy came in to give Mr. Hines a note and I thought, Gee, I wish I knew him! It was the first time I ever wanted to be in a boy's presence.

And now there were two boys I was interested in.

How absolutely incredible and marvelous to have two boyfriends!

I said to myself, hold it, Nelle Catherine. One cousin and one Mello Yello does not two boyfriends make . . . But it sure did make nice daydreaming.

* * *

The daydream lasted precisely as long as the drive to Burger King. Five minutes. Five minutes of silence on Nick's part, while I assumed he was paying attention to the traffic, and five minutes of solid joyous daydreaming on my part, whirling among a long series of boyfriends.

Nick held the glass door for me to go in first and I was aware of the way he stood way back to hold it, as if he were making absolutely sure that I couldn't brush against him. It was the first clue. I began to feel little pricks of nervousness all over.

Then we got up to the order counter and Nick stopped to look in his wallet. The way he did it, and the time he spent, turned the pricks into nails. "Let me pay for myself," I said. "After all, it's not really a date."

"Right," he said, looking relieved. "Okay." And he placed an order for himself only.

I could hardly manage to speak out loud to the girl waiting for my order. I wanted to request no onions and no pickle, but I couldn't find the words and I said nothing. I could take them out when we sat down. Okay, Nelle Catherine, I said to myself, you said it, he didn't. It isn't a date. Now just enjoy yourself anyway. If he can be polite, so can you.

And who should be sitting at a table for four and waving madly at us to join them but Holly and Chuck Summers. Chuck called hello and there was absolutely nothing we could do but sit with them.

Suddenly I was terribly ashamed of all the gossiping Holly and I had done about Nick. She knew so much of what I felt about him. I also knew what she really thought about Chuck. It didn't seem funny. It seemed rotten and wrong, to have whispered so much to each other when the boys didn't even know.

I introduced the boys. Chuck stood up, as if he were a businessman, although Nick was the one who looked like one, in his suit. It was such an adult gesture. It made me feel even more as if I were going to sit with a stranger. Or a pair of them.

And Nick actually looked at Chuck's extended right hand and ignored it and sat down on the opposite side of the booth without shaking it. "Nick Nearing," he said, "Nancy's cousin."

I wanted to scream that we weren't cousins, that we had nothing in common but a peculiar name that was probably only coincidence. We were on a date, didn't he understand? A date I'd dreamed about — but after all, the dream was just on my side. Nick had come for college interviews and a free room for the night. Still, he could have shaken Chuck's hand. It bothered me that he hadn't.

Chuck sat down and began on his french fries as if he hadn't noticed a thing.

"So," said Holly brightly, after an odd look at me, "we've heard so much about you, Nick."

Nick gave her a tight smile and bit into his cheeseburger.

I could not possibly have taken a bite.

Chuck said, "That's real interesting about you two being long-lost cousins. Everybody's talking about it. Imagine finding a girlfriend through a cookbook. Better than those computer dating services, huh?"

Nick finished chewing. "Cousin," he said very firmly, dispelling any image Chuck might have had of girl- and boyfriend.

My stomach was tied so tightly I could not possibly fit any food there. I pressed the rim of my drink cup to my lips to have something to do.

"So, Nick," said Holly again. "Tell us about yourself. You, ah, let me see, came up here for college interviews?"

Nick nodded and went on eating.

Chuck said to me, "I hear you're on the yearbook committee."

"Yes. It's going to be hard work."

Holly said, "I'm glad I'm not on it."

And that was the end of that topic. After a while Chuck said, "You play any sports, Nick? What are you going to be doing this summer?"

"Working," said Nick. He got up to shove his papers in the trash receptacle.

Holly gave me an incredulous look. I could read it perfectly. "*This* is the famous Nicholas Charles Nearing?" she was asking me.

"He's tired," I whispered. "Long trip."

Holly didn't buy that for a moment, but she pretended to.

I was not at all surprised when Chuck said, "Well, we have to be going. I've got to change before the dance. You going back to change, too, Nick? It's pretty informal. I mean, nobody else'll be wearing a suit."

"It isn't one of my goals," said Nick, in his

perfectly awful tape-recorded tone, "to be like everybody else."

"Uh huh," said Chuck, which I thought under the circumstances was very verbal of him. "Well. Nice meeting you. See you later, okay?"

But if Nick thought it was nice meeting Chuck and Holly, he didn't say so. So much for the young man with the lovely manners. My cheeks burned. I watched Holly and Chuck leave the restaurant. I knew that whatever other problems they might have together, they weren't going to lack for conversation once they got out of earshot.

"Do you feel okay?" I said to Nick. If he was coming down with mononucleosis, that would be a good excuse for his behavior.

"Yes."

"Listen, let's forget about going to the dance. I know you're tired from all that driving."

"What's the matter? Just because I found your friends boring, Nancy, you don't want to go to this dance?"

I realized just how little I knew Nick, really. What were a few silly hours spent together joking about antiques and relatives? This guy was just plain rude.

He was also the guy I wanted terribly to get to know better.

I didn't know what to do or say.

"Well, let's go home and you can change, at least," I said.

"I didn't bring jeans after all."

I could not, absolutely could not, go to an informal dance with somebody rude and tape-recorded who was wearing a vested suit.

"Let's go," he said, with all the eagerness with which one might address one's Army recruitment officer.

I had pictured us laughing and talking and dancing — the perfect couple — matching from their names to their personalities, like a splash in a glimmering pool.

It was beginning to look instead as if we were the stone going to the bottom.

Eleven

Everybody who knew me came over to be introduced. Nick, wearing such unexpected adult clothing, would sort of bow, and say "Good evening" in that awful canned tour guide voice. My friends would start to laugh, thinking he was imitating somebody, or joking. Then they'd see he wasn't trying to be funny, he was really like that; they'd look at me incredulously and then shrug and back off.

Nick wouldn't dance, either. Twice we actually got out on the dance floor. He sort of twitched a few times and then said he didn't feel like it after all and walked away. It was either walk after him or go on dancing alone. I almost deserted him. I have never been so embarrassed. I just wanted to crawl away and never be seen in public again.

Nick and I sat on the sidelines like a pair of wallflowers and had nothing to say to each other. My metal folding chair was more companionable than Nick. I felt stiff all evening. Not just my conversation, but even my face and my fingers and my legs were stiff. The few people who stayed and tried to make conversation with us gave up fairly soon, because Nick just wouldn't participate.

He gave no clues as to what was making him behave this way. All I knew was that it was, without doubt, the worst evening of my life. Everybody else seemed to be having an extraordinarily good time. Maybe it was just the comparison with Nick and me, but I ached with envy seeing everybody I knew laughing, dancing, and hugging.

Finally, at nine-thirty (the dance lasted until midnight) I said, "Nick, you must be exhausted. You want to go home?"

"All right."

It felt as if the entire student body was turning around to watch us leave. I knew they knew we weren't going to park somewhere. We were failures and they knew it and they were going to gossip about it. So much for Nancy's super cousin. If that was her idea of a good date—whew! Sure, he was good looking, but so are department store mannequins.

I blushed, thinking about their exchanges after we were gone.

Nick walked too fast for me and I had to trot to keep up with him. That was the final insult, that I had to run to keep up with somebody I wished I'd never come with! The only good thing I could think of in the entire evening (my mother always combats depression by coming up with silver linings; I guess I've picked up the habit) was that school lasted a mere five more days so there was a limit to the amount of teasing I'd have to endure. By next year maybe everybody but me would have forgotten about Nick.

Nick opened the jeep door for me, which somehow surprised me, as I had figured every remnant of his manners was long gone, and I clambered into the car.

He got in without looking at me or speaking to me, started the engine, and headed for the apartment.

Fastening my seat belt was a more complex endeavor than usual. My stiff fingers wouldn't cooperate and I was having to fight a real urge to cry. I studied the lock mechanism. Was there any way I could salvage the evening? Bring back the pleasant, funny Nicholas I'd fallen for?

Or did that Nick perhaps not exist?

"Nancy?" he said finally.

"Mmmm?" I was too upset to say much. My throat hurt. It was ridiculous. I hadn't had a sore throat from germs since I was a little kid, and here I was with my whole throat aching and rasping just because Nick hadn't made the impression I'd anticipated.

It's not important, I told myself. But it *was* important! I was crazy about Nick. I wanted other people to see the Nick I knew, not some difficult, fake, infuriating store mannequin of a jerk.

"I'm lost," said Nick, his voice not taped this time, but very tight and strained. "Where's your place from here?"

I looked up. We were on some narrow street

without street lamps or signs. "I don't recognize this," I said. "Keep driving until the next intersection and then I'll tell you."

It seemed to take forever to reach the next intersection. When we finally stopped at a stop sign and I squinted to read the road names, I'd never heard of them. "Oh, honestly, Nick," I said irritably.

"Why didn't you tell me where to go?" he said twice as irritably.

"Believe me, I wanted to, after the way you behaved!" I snapped.

"You should have given me instructions on manners to be used in front of nosy old school friends, I guess, huh?"

"I never thought you'd need a lesson in manners. You're seventeen years old. You ought to know how to shake hands by now."

We glared at each other. I know if there had been anything handy to throw, I'd have heaved it at Nick. He broke the tension by shifting into first and leaving the intersection. "Where are you going?" I demanded.

"I have no idea."

We barreled along for a mile or two and I recognized nothing. It began to strike me as very funny, in an enraging sort of way. "Stop at a gas station or something, Nick," I said. "I'll have to ask for directions. Wherever we are, I've never driven here before."

Nick turned so fast into the parking lot of a Quik-Stop Store that I'd have fallen off the seat if it weren't for the seat belt. He jerked to a stop and turned off the engine as if he wanted to snap the key. I looked at him for a minute but he didn't look at me, and finally I got out of the jeep and went inside for directions. It turned out that we were only six blocks from an entrance to the interstate, so getting home would be easy after all.

Right next to the cash register was an ice cream freezer with a glass lid, so you could look inside at all the goodies and forget your budget and make a spur-of-the-moment buy. I have always found food to be a nice way to solve problems (one reason why I'm an inch larger at the waist than I ought to be) so I decided to buy each of us an ice cream sandwich. If nothing more, it would soothe my aching throat and keep my hands busy.

I climbed back into the jeep with Nick and told him how to get us home. "But there's no rush. Here, have an ice cream sandwich. It's so hot tonight they're already melting." I gave him a paper napkin the friendly clerk had handed me and began unwrapping mine. Nick took his reluctantly, as if it were a test paper, and let it melt into his napkin.

"Nick?" I said. "What is the matter with you? I thought we were going to have such a good time and I was looking forward to it. You were such fun the other times we got together." I had more to say but Nick turned his head and looked out his window so I stopped and bit into the ice cream. The chocolate sides tasted like cardboard.

"Listen," said Nick, irritating me all over again. What did he think I was going to do? Turn deaf? "I . . . I . . ." He let out his breath hard, not a sigh so much as a slug of air. "I guess it was cutting my hair. I've felt like somebody else since eleven o'clock this morning. I cut it for the wrong reasons at the wrong time. To make an impression on people. To be different from what I really am. To please some dumb college interviewer who probably only does the interviews because he's not good enough to teach. To please friends of yours I've never met, don't care about, won't meet again. I felt . . . I don't know . . . I felt sort of open at the back. My Achilles heel, or something."

My anger felt like flour, sifting. One minute it was a big white lump and the next moment it was gone, drifting away. I tried to think of what to say to tell him I understood, but somehow I wanted to touch him more than speak to him. Only I couldn't touch him — he was way over on the other side of the jeep, frozen in on himself, and I wasn't sure how he would feel, being touched. I struggled to find words and none came.

Nick said, "You don't know what I've been through over that hair, Nancy. Since I was thirteen years old, I've gotten hassled for not cutting my hair and I know it sounds silly, but that hair mattered."

I could see how it mattered, but I couldn't see how it made him rude to dozens of people and unable to dance and unable to be pleasant. I was torn between wanting to hug him and tell him even if he was a dumb turkey with a missing ponytail I was crazy about him, and wanting to lecture him about how rotten he was.

It's odd how not having the right words can actually hurt. I felt as if I were having appendicitis. In a way I wished I *could* have an attack of it. Then I'd have a really good excuse for leaving the dance and for Nick being surly!

Although it could hardly be an excuse for Nick unless he were the one to have the appendicitis.

By the time I had written off that idea and told myself to lean over and kiss him for confiding in me, Nick had started the jeep and was heading for the interstate.

You couldn't just go ahead and hug him, could you? I thought, as furious with myself now as I had been with Nick. You had to think about it, and weigh the pros and cons, and deliberate as if it were a presidential debate. When he opened up and said personal things you just sat there like a lump, and he had no way to know what you thought or whether you cared. Now you've blown it.

"I understand about your hair," I said.

The sentence sounded remarkably stupid, five minutes after Nick had referred to his hair. He did not even look at me. I could imagine how much he regretted giving me any explanation at all.

"I mean, it's okay," I said. "It's only hair. Turn left. No, not here, at the red light. The next red light, I'm sorry. Yes, here."

"It's *not* only hair," said Nick.

"Turn again here. Right. Yes, right here, turn right. I know it isn't only hair, Nick. I understood what you were saying — left here, around that traffic circle when you get to that arrow."

In his tape-recorded voice, as if he'd flicked a switch to get to it, Nick said, "I'd rather not discuss it any further."

"Oh, talk like a normal human being, will you?" I snapped.

He left that intersection so fast the tires screamed as if we were braking instead of accelerating. In a moment we were at the apartment and my date, my wonderful date, was over.

Final Fling, I thought. It certainly was.

I got out of the jeep. Nick went up the three flights of stairs as if he were going to prison. I was surprised he didn't just get in the jeep and drive away. Probably didn't have the money for a motel and didn't want to ruin his precious three-piece suit by sleeping in it.

Any other date would have gone home, and I could have unwound by screaming in the closet, or weeping in my pillow, or dancing by myself to records. But this one had to be spending the night with us.

Mother could not have been more astonished to see us home at ten o'clock. She gave us a long look, as if we were a checkbook that she had to balance. "There's a good movie on," she said. "Robert Redford and Barbra Streisand. I'll make some popcorn. We can watch that till bedtime."

So we sat, silently, watching a very complex movie all of us had seen before. It was the sort of film that makes you sad and full of understanding for two people who will just never match except at the edges, and the edges will always be raw.

I thought about our evening. If I had just had more experience with boys — dated a lot, been popular — I'd have been able to handle Nick. He had been under a lot of pressure, and I shouldn't have dragged him to a function where things could only get worse. I should have known enough to forget it and go home after that horrendous meal with Chuck and Holly. And the one chance to make things better, in the Quick-Stop parking lot (how unromantic could a place be?), I'd messed up by snapping at him.

The three of us sat chewing popcorn. When you really chew popcorn — instead of crunching it, laughing, reaching for another handful, passing the towel to mop your greasy fingers, laughing about that too — things are pretty bad.

Bedtime was horrible. Mother and I made up the couch and Nick stood there looking as if he were a non-somniac with no sleep requirements. When the lights were out and all the awkward good nights had been said, I quietly shut my bedroom door. I pulled the covers up in spite of the heat, put my head under my pillow, and cried.

Twelve

When I woke up Saturday morning I heard the unfamiliar sounds of a third person in our apartment, shuffling around, and getting up. Everything looks better in the morning. That morning I felt more than able to have a waffle with Nick, smile at him, make friends again, and get rid of the bad taste of the evening before. I hopped out of bed, throwing the sheets back and making it quickly before I did anything else. I hate an unmade bed. It's the only thing I'm always neat about.

Then I remembered that my hairbrush was in the bathroom. My bathrobe was in the bathroom. My toothbrush was in the bathroom. To get to them I'd have to go past Nick in the living room. I took a look at myself in the dressing table mirror. My hair was bumpy rather than wavy. My cheeks were wrinkled from the pillow and my eyes were puffy from last night's crying. And my nightgown. My nightgown was a joke gift from mother last year. It was short and brilliant pink and in purple glittering letters astride a forked symbol, it said KILLER WOMAN!

I moaned softly, pulling open a bureau drawer to see what else I could throw on. There was a long undershirt style nightie with a profile of the Incredible Hulk on it. There was last year's bathrobe with the sleeve torn out on the left side that I'd never mended because it didn't fit me anymore and why mend something you can't wear, right?

"Nancy?" called Mother. "Nick's finishing up his breakfast. He's leaving in a moment. Don't you want to say good-bye?"

"No," I said. "I mean — yes, I do want to say good-bye, but I'm not up yet."

"Then get up," she said reasonably enough.

"No, no," said Nick hastily on the other side of the door. "It's really early. And this is Saturday, you two would be sleeping late if it weren't for me. I have to run. Thanks a lot for everything, Mrs. Nearing, I won't impose on you again like this."

Well, that settled that. I stopped trying to pull on my jeans and shirt to get out there in time to say good-bye. He wouldn't impose on us again like this.

I wondered why he could talk so easily with Mother. "Good-bye, Nick," I called. "Good luck on your interviews."

"Thanks." His feet were much noisier than Mother's. He sounded like a thudding giant. Her soft patter followed him to the door. "Good-bye, Nick. Drive carefully. Come again."

"Yes, ma'am," he said, though whether he

meant to drive carefully or come again I couldn't tell. And then the door closed behind him.

I got back in bed. Who wanted to face a day like today, filled with all the things I should have said and could have done and ought to have been?

I listened to Mother getting herself another cup of coffee. There was an abrupt end to the gurgle of the percolator. She'd unplugged it.

"Nannie?" she said, knocking on my door. "May I come in?"

She had never asked permission to come into my room before. It made me feel terribly sad, as if I had crossed some line into a bleak life where people had to tiptoe around each other, worrying about hurting each other.

Oh, good grief, Nelle Catherine, I told myself. So a spoiled seventeen-year-old boy ruins your evening by being stuffy and stupid about his dumb hair. So he explains it to you and you ruin your chance to show him you care and you understand. So that's going to ruin your Saturday?

Yes, I told myself, yes, it's going to ruin my Saturday. Not to mention all my daydreams about Nicholas Charles Nearing. "Sure, Mother, come on in."

She sat on my bed looking at me as she sipped her coffee. Mother drinks it black. It makes me gag even to think of black coffee. She set her cup down on the night table. "Roll over, sweetheart. I'll give you a backrub."

I *love* backrubs. If I were being executed and they gave me one last request, it would probably be for a backrub. I flopped on my stomach and

Mother began kneading my back. "So what happened?" she said softly. "Pretty bad?"

We had joked a lot about boys. Exchanged quips about looking at boys and thinking about boys and drawing boys in sketch pads. But we'd never actually talked about boys: what they thought, or wanted, or needed. Even with Holly and Ginger, I don't think I had ever done more than gossip about boys: who was dating whom, and was he or she worth that attention.

But I found myself telling Mother everything. From the taped voice syndrome to the getting lost and the haircut bit and the insults exchanged.

Mother stopped massaging my back and started in on her coffee again. By that time it must have been cold. The only thing worse than black coffee would certainly be cold black coffee.

"He really was embarrassed, wasn't he?" she said. "I thought of Nick as being a bit more smooth than that, but I suppose seventeen is really pretty young. He just got thrown a few more curve balls than he was ready for."

"Embarrassed?" I said. "Curve balls? Like what, Mother?"

"Oh, Nancy, how much could go wrong for a boy?"

"How much could go wrong for a girl?" I countered.

She laughed and patted me. "Look. He was wearing the wrong clothes. Nobody likes wearing the wrong thing in public."

"But he didn't have to wear them. We could have come back to change."

"He was feeling contrary, I guess. He probably

didn't realize just how obvious and foolish he'd feel in a vested suit when every other boy was in jeans. And he'd had that haircut. I'm amazed he confessed so much to you about his feelings about that. But obviously he felt silly and different from top to bottom."

"Believe me, he acted it, too."

"And then he got lost driving home. What red-blooded American boy enjoys confessing to his date that he's lost?"

That I could see. I hadn't at the time, it had just irritated me, but now I could see that he must have been humiliated by getting lost. "But, Mother," I said, "what were these curve balls he got sent? I don't understand what you meant by that. The college interviews? My friends at the dance? He must have been ready for that stuff."

"You," she said.

"What about me?"

"He told you twice, Nannie. A cousin is not like a regular girl. After all, honey, Nick has even less experience dating than you do."

It was not possible for me to think of Nick as inexperienced and unsure. He was a boy and a year older. He had everything — looks, personality, brains, body . . . and that awful voice.

"Nan, when you two left this apartment Nick started to panic and wanted me along. I didn't know whether to laugh or to cry. He expected some old girl cousin and a boring evening being polite with all her dumb old friends. Instead this beautiful slender girl with long blonde hair and an excited smile is there ready to go out with him. She's dancing around in these tight jeans thinking about a dance, and all of a sudden it's a date. He's supposed to dance with her, squire her around, make interesting conversation with her, open doors for her, maybe even kiss her — and he panicked."

I could understand panic. There were a couple of boys in the senior class whose smiles made me panic, whose greetings for some reason made it impossible for me to greet them back, although that was what I wanted to do most. But panic over *me?* "Mother, I love the adjectives you're using, but you are, as my mother, rather prejudiced. I think Nick just didn't want my company and he felt like being rotten, because it made him feel better about his rotten day to make my day rotten."

"Whew!" said Mother, laughing. "People hardly ever feel like being rotten on purpose, honey. Everybody wants to have a good time. Nobody wants friends to shrug and walk away and have to leave early and not have anything to say or share. Nick probably feels as terrible as you do. Worse, because he started it. He didn't sleep much last night. Tossed around for hours. I don't know if it was the lumps on our terrible couch or his thoughts that kept him awake, but he was pretty bleary-eyed this morning. Poor boy. And facing two more interviews, too."

I got up and went into the kitchen to have some shredded wheat. "Mother, why do you think he suddenly starts talking in that awful annoying smooth voice?"

"It may be that he thinks it's attractive. Or he may feel safe behind it. Like somebody else. Or he may not be aware of it. It may be a nervous tic. I'm sure it's just an adolescent habit. He'll outgrow it, Nancy."

Much good that would do me. I'd never see him again. How would I know if he ever outgrew the habit?

I sat over my shredded wheat. Things have to be pretty bad to sit over shredded wheat for any length of time. I told myself it didn't matter one bit to me if Nick quit talking like that. He was stupid and I didn't care.

But he wasn't stupid and I did care.

At eleven o'clock I picked up the telephone and called Rod Holmes. My second time calling a boy. It might be as much of an error as the first time, but I could not face a weekend of just sitting there running my mind over my ought to haves and should have dones.

"Rod?" I said. "Nancy. You want to bicycle out to the waterfall and have a picnic?"

Mother gaped at me. I guess she thought I was calling Holly or Ginger. But nothing would be worse than them, today. They'd want to dissect Nick, and I couldn't face that. Not until I knew what I felt about Nick first.

"Great idea," said Rod instantly. "I'll meet you in forty-five minutes. I'll bring potato chips and soft drinks if you'll bring sandwiches."

It was so easy! As if we had done this several times before, and had known before the phones rang what we'd be doing this time. Why hadn't it been that easy with Nick?

"My goodness," said my mother, shaking her head. "Two weeks ago, nothing would have made you do that."

"I'm sick of just thinking about boys, Mother. Rod likes me. I need somebody who likes me, after last night."

"Nick likes you," she said. "A lot."

"Right," I said sarcastically. "So much he can't dance or speak with me. Now, do we have any ham or do I have to make peanut butter and jelly?"

Peanut butter and jelly conjured up the memory of that really nice night with Nick. Last night was pretty painful compared to that night. I made ham sandwiches, found some pickles and a few Oreo cookies, and dropped them in my little backpack. Tying a red bandanna over my hair, I ran down the stairs to get my bike from the storeroom.

I didn't feel happy yet, but at least I was doing something, and Rod would be good company. I didn't think Rod would object to being chosen as a friend in time of need, rather than a date.

Thirteen

"I don't think we should sit there, Nance," said Rod, when I set my backpack down on a large, flat, sunbaked rock with a perfect view of the waterfall. "Snakes are out in this heat," he said. "I don't see any, but I'd rather not chance it."

I jumped about a foot.

Rod grinned. "I'm not trying to be difficult. I just hate snakes. Let's go over to the picnic grove and eat there."

We locked the bicycles together and chained one to a little sapling and then walked through the woods to the picnic area. The park was new. Fifty-five acres along the river's edge had been donated to the town by the hosiery mill, when they finally realized they were never going to build there. The Cub, Boy, and Girl Scouts had spent three years carving trails through the woods and over the meadows, building tables and shelters, and painting trash receptacles in woodsy colors, like wartime camouflage. I had never been a Scout. When I saw how much they'd accomplished I found myself wishing I had been part of it all, instead of out toting Mother hither and yon in search of the perfect antique.

"How was the dance last night?" Rod asked.

"Horrible. My cousin was a complete jerk. We left early and he got lost driving home and we ended up spending the evening in front of the television."

Rod laughed. "Poor guy. Getting lost in this little burg. Bet he feels like a jerk today, too. What was horrible about the dance?"

"The dance was probably fine. It was my cousin." Funny — I didn't feel at all cousinly toward Nick. I really wanted to say "my date," but Nick had made it pretty clear he wasn't my date, so that didn't seem the right word either.

"What did you watch? That Barbra Streisand thing? I like that movie. You really want them to live happily ever after, but all along you can see they never will. They are too different. It makes you worry about the sort of person you'll fall in love with, you know?"

I choked on the pickle I was nibbling. "Yes, I know."

"Are you choking?"

"Yes," I gasped, "but only a little."

Rod whacked me on the back, almost dislocating my vertebrae. "That's not what you do for choking anymore," I said. "You make a fist in the person's stomach, and jerk the fist hard into his abdomen to kind of whomp the choke out of him from the bottom up."

"Oh, really? Show me." Rod's eyes glinted and he was half grinning.

I put my hands around his waist and pressed my fist into his stomach.

"You're not pushing hard enough Nance. That doesn't even flatten my belly button."

I was suddenly too embarrassed to do it any more and I broke away, blushing, but it was a different kind of blush from the painful ones of last night. We ate facing each other, chewing ham sandwiches and crunching potato chips and then just sort of giggling. I felt silly and stupid but I was enjoying myself tremendously. I couldn't think of anything at all to say, but it didn't seem to matter. Giggling and eating were plenty for Rod. After lunch we retrieved our bikes and rode all up and down the Scout trails. We chased each other, vaulted our bikes over one fallen log (it was a stick; we just called it a log to sound more adventurous), and pretended to find snakes in the tree limbs so we could rescue each other from certain death. I felt about nine years old. I couldn't believe we were really playing in the woods like this, and yet it was so much fun.

"I have to go," said Rod suddenly. "I've already started my summer job and I'm due there at three."

It was like the end of Mary Poppins's laughing gas. "Oh," I said.

We rode solemnly out of the park. "What's your summer job?" I asked.

"Information desk at the hospital. Three to eleven shift. I log visitors in and out. I tell them what room their friends are in. How many can go in at a time. Where X-ray is. Where the gift shop is. When the city bus leaves. The work is boring and yet I really love it. All those people moving past me, Nancy, wrapped up in lives I don't know anything about. Everybody is worried and tense and concerned, unless they're there to see newborn babies. It's amazing to think of all these people leading their lives and you aren't part of them at all. They don't even know you exist. Even when you tell them how to find the elevator to Memorial West Wing third floor they don't really see you. It makes you feel half visible."

"You like that feeling?"

"I don't like it or dislike it. It's a watcher's feeling. I want to be a journalist, you know, and I think that's the kind of sensation journalists must have a lot. Standing there watching and thinking and taking notes while other people's lives whisk by."

I had never been anywhere really except school. I began to think of how much I was missing, not getting out in the world, not seeing the lives of all those other people whisking by. I said, "But if you want to be a journalist, how come you didn't get a summer job at the newspaper?"

"Oh, wow!" Rod shook his head, grinning at the dusty ground. "Forget that! Everybody wants a summer job at the paper and there aren't any. Besides, my father says I have to have wide experience so I can make intelligent analyses of the stories I write."

"Wide experience," I repeated. "Is hospital work wide?"

"Well, it's a wedge. What I want is to have a

resume like you read on the jackets of spy novels. Where the writer has paddled a canoe in northern Canada, studied archaeology in Crete, taught mathematics in Paraguay, tended bar in San Diego, been a hang-glider instructor off the Outer Banks, repaired pre-1910 electric automobiles, and taken advanced degrees in Manchurian dialects."

"I like to see a person with a few goals," I said, laughing. How interesting people were, once you talked to them! Who would have thought Rod Holmes wanted all that? That wild, different excitement-packed life! It made me embarrassed about my own daydreams, which consisted of little goals, such as holding hands, going steady, getting kissed . . .

I sighed. Everybody but me had his act together.

"You have a summer job?" asked Rod.

"Couldn't find one."

"There aren't any more paying jobs left at the hospital, but I'll tell you, Nancy, they're desperate for volunteers," said Rod seriously. "Nobody volunteers anymore. All the women who used to be able to give an afternoon a week have gone back to work and they're too tired to come in evenings. It's rough down there, without the volunteers filling in."

"What do volunteers do?"

"Oh, they take patients down to X-ray and walk them after their surgery and exchange their library books and water their flowers. It sounds rinky-dink, but nobody likes to wait four hours for X-ray and then go in alone. Especially if the patient has to go to the bathroom, or something."

Waiting four hours outside X-ray with a patient who needed to go to the bathroom didn't sound too good. But I did need something to do all summer, and after hearing all the things Rod wanted to do I felt sort of ashamed for not wanting to do more myself. "How do I sign up?" I said.

"Come down with me right now. I'll introduce you to the lady in charge of volunteers."

"Nancy," said Mrs. Perkins, "we'd love to have you. How many hours can you work? Can you start Monday — day after tomorrow? We need workers everywhere. You can choose flowers, library, transportation, gift shop, linens — you name it."

"I think I'd like to be with people," I said, "moving around. Not . . . not stuck in some room somewhere." I felt nervous saying that so bluntly but Mrs. Perkins nodded. "Just the way I feel. I hate this office. Walls between me and all the action. How about flowers? There's plenty of action there. You rush around with a little metal cart taking the flowers from the delivery drop up to each room. You get to chat with the patients and their families. Receiving flowers always cheers people up and that will make you feel good about what you're doing."

"Okay. Flowers sound fine. Are there really enough deliveries to keep me busy?"

"Oh, yes. You'll be scurrying around every minute. And if by some chance you run out of things to do, they always need help in the gift shop."

We settled on four afternoons, from noon till

six. Mrs. Perkins gave me a funny little smile. "Most people just work one afternoon a week," she said. "You may find your enthusiasm dwindles after a bit. Feel free to come back if you want a change, Nancy. Now. Wear a dress and stockings and comfortable shoes. Not sneakers. We used to have uniforms, but we dropped that. You'll just wear a bright pink apron. See you Monday!"

I rode my bicycle home and the world I passed looked a lot better. It was very hot, but there was a breeze, and I made another breeze of my own, zooming along on my bike. The hospital happened to be a nice distance from home and on roads where biking was fairly safe. Even if we did get a car, I'd ride my bike. Keep me trim all summer.

I would not call Rod a second time. It was his turn now.

I hoped he would call me, and yet I wasn't counting on it. Nice as Rod was — and he was *very* nice — I didn't feel about him the way I had about Nick.

I wished I did. Nick was difficult and mysterious and sulky and far away. What good was a crush on Nick? Why couldn't I be crazy about Rod, who was interesting and funny and easy and close by?

I rode halfway up the big hill before I could no longer push the pedals down. I dismounted and walked the rest of the way up. I could not write Nick off, much as I wanted to. He was right there, filling up my thoughts.

Oh, Nelle Catherine, I said to myself, puffing at the top of the hill. Some guy you met three times, you're going to go into a decline over? Come on, lady. He's not worth it.

I coasted down the other side of the hill and into the little cramped parking lot of our apartment. Mother and I were going to spend the afternoon car shopping. We had pretty well decided that a new car was not for us. We could save thousands of dollars by buying a good used model. Of course, we wouldn't get very good gas mileage, but the car would run. We'd have our freedom back. Life without a car in a town as spread out as ours is not much fun.

The car in our space was not a new one Mother was trying out.

It was Nick's jeep.

Fourteen

"Hello, Nancy."

"Oh, hi, Nick."

His presence seemed to swirl about me. Rod had been a friend, relaxing and fun. Nick was more than I could think about at one time.

"Did you forget something?" I said. Now it was *my* voice that sounded tape-recorded! I tried to control it and get it back to normal.

"Yes." Nick looked so unbelievably handsome. He was wearing the blue jeans he'd told me he hadn't brought and a striped shirt with an open collar. He looked terrific. I swallowed.

"What did you forget?" I said. "I'll go up and look for it."

He moved between me and the apartment building door. "I . . . ah . . . I forgot to apologize for last night."

He was about three or four inches taller than I was. I looked up at him. He was squinting into the late afternoon sun, and it gave him a pinched tense look. At least, I hoped it was the sun.

"That's all right," I said, and to my relief my voice was perfectly calm and normal. Wouldn't it be awful if Nick's retread voice were infectious! "Some evenings just don't work out that well. I wasn't much to boast about either. It's hot, isn't it? You want to come in and have some iced tea? I'm dying of thirst, myself. I've been outdoors all day. How were the interviews? Did you like the colleges? Did they like you?"

Now I was babbling. I decided the absolutely worst thing about learning to be with a boy you liked was talking. Rod wanted to be a hang-gliding instructor. I just wanted to be able to talk.

I unlocked the apartment. Mother wasn't home, which seemed good at first, but in a moment I realized it meant I'd have to do all the talking to Nick myself. "Want sugar?" I said, words pouring out of me like water from a faucet. "Or lemon? Both? I take it with both. Mother takes it plain, without anything, that is, because she likes it that way. How's your father, anyway?"

Nick had been listening to me with his mouth slightly open, as if he had a sentence ready but no place to put it. I flushed. "I like mine plain, too, thanks. My father's fine. I guess the interviews were okay. I don't know how to tell. Have to wait until I hear from them, I guess. Listen, I'm sorry about last night. I don't know what happened. I just couldn't make myself be pleasant. You were right, I could have. I just didn't, and I'm sorry."

I handed him his glass of tea. The outside

was wet with condensation and it slid out of my hand into his. I dried my hand on a towel and handed him a napkin. The only thing I could think of to say were Mother's explanations for his behavior. "You behaved strangely because you were with this beautiful, romantic, slender girl in tight jeans," I thought — but I didn't say it out loud. I didn't say anything. It was as bad as last night. There was so much to be said that there was nowhere to begin. It made my chest hurt. I could not understand why not being able to talk would be so painful, physically painful. Finally I said, "Why didn't you just tell me how much you didn't want to go out, and then we'd have been spared all that."

"I didn't know I didn't want to until I got there."

"Kind of like a final exam, huh?"

"It even felt like an exam, Nancy. Your friends grilling me about who and what I am. That Holly. I had the feeling she knew everything about me from my brand of underwear to my phone number."

"I'm sorry, Nick. She didn't quite know that much, but I had talked about you a lot and she was looking forward to meeting you."

Nick seemed puzzled by this, as if I were contradicting something. "I thought you just asked me on the spur of the moment, when I called about coming up for those interviews."

"Well," I said, turning scarlet (the color Mother wanted her walls to be, not her daughter), "it was sort of a big spur and a long moment."

"Really? I thought you were just trying to,

you know, entertain the cousin when he's in town mooching a meal."

"Nick!" I was really hurt. How could he think that?

But then, I had said nothing to indicate how much the evening meant to me. Had I expected him to figure out by osmosis that I was crazy about him? I choked on my tea — my second choke of the day. He looked at me strangely. "Just went down the wrong way," I said, and I hoped fervently I would not start hiccuping, which I often do when I'm nervous and drinking something cold and sitting in the draft of the air conditioner.

"So did last night," he said ruefully. He twirled his glass on his palm. "I hate for new cousins to part on bad terms. Can we try again tonight?"

"Try again?" I said. Why did he have to say *cousins*? I didn't want to be his cousin. I'd had enough of this relative business. I wanted to be his date.

"A movie or something? Bowling? Dinner?"

"I thought you were broke," I said.

Nick's features were tense again, and I thought, why didn't I just answer him? Why did I delay giving him an answer, tease him, string it out? I hate it when people do that to me! "I mean, I'd love to," I said, and for once I managed some of the words I wanted to use. "I don't want to be just cousins. If you want to ask me on a date, I'd love to go. Although I thought you were broke and needed everything for college, so we can just sit here and watch television if you'd rather."

Nick looked at the ceiling where the old basket hooks still hung, waiting, I guess, for another generation of little old baskets. "I am sort of poor," he said. "but I have plenty of money. I'm saving it for important things, but I'd take you out anyway." He looked appalled. "I didn't mean that, Nancy, not the way it sounded. I want to spend the money, it's not that you're not important, it . . . Jeez, it was easier to talk to you when you were a long-lost cousin, Nancy."

"Cousins," I said, starting to laugh, "I don't need."

"Need a date for tonight?"

"Very much."

It seemed logical to get a little closer, which we did. I had never kissed, not real long happy kisses. It was like being under water. I kept thinking, I'm going to suffocate if I don't figure out how to breathe and be with Nick at the same time.

I was just getting the hang of it when Mother walked in.

"Now that's what I call affection," she said. "Have you written off last night?"

Nick sprang away from me as if we'd been caught doing something criminal. He blushed. Oddly enough, for the first time in my life, I didn't. I just grinned. "Cheshire cat," said Mother to me. She poured herself some iced tea and rescued our glasses. Our ice had melted down and the glasses were half full of pale gold water. "I'm having supper here," she said. "Lettuce, cauliflower, broccoli, and carrot salad. If you are attracted by that description, by all means stay. Otherwise I have a very good book to read."

"I feel thrown out," said Nick.

"I," I said to him, "feel like a pizza all the way."

"Funny, you don't look it."

It was the oldest line in the world and we both laughed insanely about it all the way to the pizza place.

The pizza wedge I was working on had an extra glop of mozzarella and little strings of cheese were hanging from the edges of my mouth down to my fingers. We were talking across a tiny scarred wooden table at a booth for two along the back wall. The only light was a stump of a candle in a smoke-stained red glass. Nick reached across and wrapped the cheese strands around his finger until he had a little wreath of white cheese on it and then I ate the cheese off his finger.

"You and your mother are coming to the family reunion in August, aren't you?"

"Nick, you know we aren't really cousins."

"We might be. I'm assuming we are. I like to think that we are. Anyway, I'm going to ask Dad to give you an official invitation."

So we were back to cousins. I decided not to make an issue of it. I took another pizza wedge instead. It's only good when it's hot.

"I'm not giving tours this summer," he said. "I memorized those talks about the furniture and the history and it got into my voice. Everybody complains about my voice and I have to kick that habit, I really do."

"You think the voice comes from giving the tours?"

"That's when I started it. I felt so silly at first, in those britches and that huge muslin shirt, talking about door lintels. When I used my fake voice it felt as if somebody else were giving the tours. I didn't feel silly anymore."

"I thought you looked neat. Especially the hair. I kind of miss your hair."

He said, "Wait till you see our battle in August. Last year I was just a member of the militia, but this year I'm the Tory captain who leads the charge. I have a really neat uniform."

"You're the Tory captain? Which side are you on, anyway?"

"The British side, obviously. As a matter of fact at the end of the battle the Revolutionaries surrender and the King's men win Nearing River House and the surrounding areas."

"We celebrate that?" I said, incensed. "I thought we only reenacted the victorious battles."

"Somebody is victorious in every battle. It just happens that this one was a Loyalist victory, and if we're going to participate in Revolutionary reenactments, that's what we've got. It's a lot of fun. My men attack the house where a small but intrepid band of Revolutionaries have taken refuge.

"I guess Revolutionaries are always intrepid."

"Absolutely. But they're not as clever as I am. Not only do I order my men to fire upon them, but I roll carts filled with burning straw against the wooden siding of Nearing River House and they are forced to surrender after several casualties on each side. I do all this whooping and hollering to goad my men into dangerous action and weep over their broken bodies and stand triumphant in the doorway at the end."

"And what does the audience do?"

"What do you mean? They enjoy it, of course."

Like me enjoying Nick. I would be the most receptive audience he ever had. "No, I mean, do they cheer or boo when the Loyalists win?"

"Oh, they just clap indiscriminately. It's late in the day for worrying about sides. Besides, most of the outsiders who come to watch it think it's a Civil War battle and that the Loyalists are Union soldiers. It's amazing how many Northerners think the only battles ever fought in the South were Civil War battles. They think of the American Revolution as this Massachusetts thing, with maybe a little New York and Saratoga and Benedict Arnold mixed in. Northerners always look confused when you tell them there was heavy decisive action in the Carolinas during the Revolution."

"You're really interested in it, aren't you?"

"I love it. My father loves the remains of history — the antiques and the tools and the buildings. I love the conflict of war. I wouldn't love a real war, you understand, I don't ever want to see one, or be in one, but wars in the past fascinate me. My favorites are World War I and the American Revolution. I read about World War I all the time."

"Are you going to major in history when you get to college?"

"No. Why pay good money to have professors tell me about things I''ll be reading about all my life? I think I'll major in math. Go into computers, or something. But I'm not really sure."

There was one cold wedge of pizza left on the round aluminum platter. Nick got up, and I almost did, too, thinking he wanted to leave, but he came around the tiny table and sat beside me. There was definitely not room for a second person. We were terribly squashed, and I loved it. Nick felt very solid next to me. I wondered if his pulse were racing like mine.

"I have to leave," he said, which I considered a totally inappropriate remark for the position we were in. "It's a long drive, I have to get going."

I sighed. "Maybe you can stop in here again on your way up to Pennsylvania this July."

"I'm not going up there this summer, remember?"

It amazed me that I could have forgotten one word Nick had ever said. I'd spent a lot of nights rerunning our conversations in my mind. "Yes, you did," I admitted, "I'd forgotten."

"My mother's pretty upset over it."

"I can imagine."

We left the pizza parlor and got back into Nick's jeep and suddenly, depressingly, we were as awkward as before. Nick not only didn't kiss me, he didn't even look at me. "Thanks for a nice evening," I said.

"Oh yes, sure," he said, negotiating a turn.

"It was nice of you to come back."

"Back?" he said, as if he'd forgotten the night before.

It made me seasick, swinging back and forth from being relaxed with each other to being strangers. I wanted him to kiss me good night and I knew he wasn't considering it, or he'd considered it and decided against it. We went up the stairs separately and he yelled for my mother to unlock the door — to prevent me, I suppose, from being able to waste time looking for my key. Time in which his cue would be a kiss.

When he left, his good-bye to my mother was as cordial as his good-bye to me. He clattered down the stairs like a man without a care in the world. I felt like a debt that had been paid off. He'd come back, apologized, behaved well, bought me a meal, and now he was done with that scene. Whew! Back home to better things.

I felt very tired that night, but I slept poorly. I kept trying to transfer my feelings from Nick, who didn't want them, to Rod, who might.

It didn't work.

Fifteen

The summer passed slowly, but pleasantly enough. It was oppressively hot. We weren't able to turn off the air conditioners at all, and my whole life was accompanied by hums and whirs of cold air.

Hospital work left me with mixed feelings. Once I took a bouquet in to a very old lady who thought I was her granddaughter. I held her curled arthritic hand and felt the thick tunnels of her veins tremble. I told her yes, I loved her, yes, Grandmother, everything will be all right, don't worry. She fell asleep after a while and I really felt good, as if I'd done something really worthwhile. But other times the same sort of room and the same sort of patient would make me feel as grim and sterile and gray as the hospital corridors. All I knew for sure was that I did not want a career in medicine.

Rod and I talked these things over at length. We went out together a great deal, and it was a lot of fun. Rod was reliably funny and nice. But we weren't going out on dates, we were friends. That was one topic we never discussed and I never could quite bring it up because I, for one, did not want the situation to change. I just wondered about it.

Why was this perfectly fine, handsome, funny boy just a friend? Why didn't either of us feel like kissing? Just remembering Nick pressed up against me in the pizza booth could make my heart race. The chemistry of this seemed unfair — to be crazy about Nick, and only fond of Rod.

In July a letter came from Nick. Addressed to me.

Dear Nancy:

Plans for the family reunion are moving right along.

We've rehearsed the battle scene enough, I'm told — once! My aunt Marge is the Historical Society President, and has been from time immemorial. She thinks it'll be so much more spontaneous and interesting if we have no idea what we're doing.

Aunt Catherine will be writing to you about where you'll be spending Friday and Saturday nights, but everything has gotten quite complex. Basically the situation is that my mother has decided that since I'm not going up to see her, she'll come down to see me. She also wants to see me in this battle, since I'm the Tory captain. She perceives the role as being some great honor; she doesn't know that when they chose parts I just happened to be standing there. It may be a sticky reunion. She and my father have not laid eyes on each other for six years, and that time was most reluctantly, at the airport, to hand me over.

I'm really nervous about her coming down, but I'm not as nervous as my father. He's getting ulcers.

Anyway, what we thought we'd do, if you and your mother can stand it, is sort of use you as buffers. We'll sleep you two and my mother and Aunt Catherine all at our house, and Dad and I will go over to Aunt Marge's. If Mom gets tense because I'm not around, I'll sleep on a sleeping bag in the living room (there is a couch, but you know these antique couches) to keep her from saying I don't love her anymore.

Aunt Catherine and Mom always got along pretty well, and your mother is a real pleasant person (she got along with me, and I wasn't pleasant) so let's hope for the best.

Let me know if this is okay, or if we should make motel reservations for you.

Your cousin,
Nick

I stuck my face into one of the pillows on the couch and screamed, "Aaaaaahhhhhh!"

Mother looked up at me a bit nervously. Understandable reaction. "Yes, dear?"

"Cousin," I explained, spitting out the consonants. "Here I am just being friends with a perfectly fine Rod Holmes and wasting time being in love with a complete dolt who thinks I'm his *cousin*. I am beginning to hate that word. You know why he wrote, Mother? He wrote because he needs somebody to absorb the shock waves his mother is going to make and he thinks you and I would be the perfect candidates." I made a long series of unintelligible noises at the pillow and ground my teeth.

"Ah hah!" said my mother, in her antique-find voice.

"What?" I looked around, but I saw no spectacular treasures lurking in our totally cleansed corners.

"I wondered about you and Nick and Rod. I never understood, and you, close-mouthed thing that you are, haven't shared a single thought with me since that morning after the Final Fling. Now I see. You expect better things out of Nick than he's prepared to give. It makes me feel like cross-stitching a motto for you."

"I don't want a motto. I want Nick."

Mother laughed. "How about: I never promised you a rose garden. Or: Life is unfair. Or maybe: Before you meet the charming prince, you have to kiss a lot of toads."

"Neither Rod nor Nick is a toad."

"Has either of them kissed you?"

"The motto I cross-stitch for you will be: Mind thine own business."

We both giggled. "Well," she said, "are we going to buffer or go to a motel?"

"Since the only reason I want to go to this reunion is to be reunited with Nick," I said, "a motel seems self-defeating."

"Since the only reason I want to go to this reunion is to finish tracking down who your father was, and I am unlikely to be able to do that from the Holiday Inn," said Mother, "I will have to agree with you. Another plus of the buffer agreement is that I can go off my diet. No more cauliflower and broccoli salads."

"What does dieting have to do with it?" I said.

"Did you ever hear of a thin buffer?" she asked me.

We giggled again and poked each other, as excited as little kids going to a birthday party. "I plan to *lose* weight before then. I intend to look terrific."

"I always say if you have to be a cousin, you may as well be the most attractive cousin of all, right?"

"Now *there's* a motto."

When we arrived at the Nearings' at a little after three on Friday, I was five pounds thinner, Mother was wearing a sundress that made her look lovely, and we were driving our brand-new five-year-old station wagon. Right up until the moment we saw the crowd of maybe fifty or sixty people milling around on the grass between the antique shop and the split-level house I was excited and eager. And then I didn't even want to get out of the car. What if I couldn't find Nick, among all these strangers, and had to wander among them trying to look as if I belonged? What if Nick came up to me with some pretty slender girl on his arm and introduced her as his girlfriend and me as his cousin? What if they had forgotten we were coming? We didn't really know any of these people, and we didn't really belong here, except for the coincidence of my initials. What if —

"Hi!" said Nick, opening the door on my side at the same instant his father opened the door on Mother's side. "We've been waiting for you."

He astonished me by kissing me immediately right in front of everybody. I didn't have time to revise my opinion of the situation because it became clear that introductions to Nearings involved kisses and hugs with Nearings; Mother and I were festooned with kisses and hugs like Christmas trees with popcorn.

"And this is my cousin Maude," said Nick, and Maude kissed both my cheeks. "And her husband Dirk." Dirk kissed me on the forehead. He asked if it was true that Nick had cut his hair for me and I said no, I didn't think so. Dirk and Maude laughed and passed me on to Mrs. Earl. "Soon to become a Nearing," she explained. "I'm marrying Nick's uncle Stephen."

"I don't have an uncle Stephen," said Nick, frowning.

"Yes, you do," said Mrs. Earl impatiently, hugging me at the same time. I felt like a library book, being taken in and out. "Marcia's brother."

"Oh, him. He's my cousin Eric's uncle — he's hardly related to me at all. Go ahead and marry him."

They made friendly faces at her and Mrs. Earl was lost in a swirl of Nearings. I said, "If he's your cousin Eric's uncle, why isn't he related to you much at all?"

"Because Eric is about a third cousin twice removed. I don't know Eric either. If I have to introduce you to some man and I don't say his name because I've forgotten it, it's probably Eric."

Another couple bobbed up in front of me. "Cousin Sue, Cousin Arnold, this is Nancy Nearing."

Sue was about twenty and expecting to deliver another Nearing that very day, from the look of her. We beamed at each other, but with the unborn Nearing between us hugging was out. Arnold kissed me twice instead. "They get prettier every year, don't they, Nick?" he said.

Relatives came and went like the tide.

"How do you keep them all straight?" I said to Nick.

"I don't try. I just call them all cousin."

"Do we get an intermission, or does this go on steadily until Sunday afternoon?"

"It sort of goes in cycles. Like phases of the moon. There'll be these big swells of people you haven't met since last year and then they'll fade away and be replaced by another batch. No coffee breaks allowed. From here on in, it's solid cousinry."

A great big bear of a man came up, put his arm around me, and kissed the top of my head. "So this is Nancy," he said. "You're the one who convinced Nick to cut his hair ahead of schedule. I've been looking forward to meeting you, little lady."

Nick had on the sort of smile that meant his taped voice would come on soon.

"I knew you'd have to be attractive," said the bear, "and you are. Congratulations, Nick. You were a little shy about entering the race, but you've —"

"And this is my mother," I said loudly.

"Eleanor Nearing. Perhaps you knew my father, Robert."

The bear immediately took the bait and entered a long discussion about the various Roberts in the Nearing clan. Nick and I withdrew. In fact, we withdrew so much I began to wonder if we were getting an intermission after all. We ended up way behind the split-level at the back of the flower garden, which was just a huge golden blur of marigolds, in a little grove of high bush blueberries. "I see you've been getting all the expected static about having your hair cut."

"I'm used to it now."

"The short hair or the static?"

"The short hair. I've gotten static all my life."

There was nothing to sit down on. We stood awkwardly and looked at each other. My hands had been so useful in shaking relatives' hands but now they dangled around with nothing to do. I wanted to hug Nick but my arms couldn't quite bring themselves to do it. So they hung there, like separate people, arguing with each other.

"Tonight is a dinner at the Barbecue House," said Nick. "Do you like barbecue?"

"Actually I'd rather have one of your famous peanut butter and jelly sandwiches." He kind of smiled. He was so handsome, standing there. I thought about what the bear had said to him: *You were a little shy* . . . I said, "What's on the agenda for tomorrow besides the battle?"

"Southern-style breakfast at nine. Ham, biscuits, grits, sausage, and so forth. Genealogy exchanges from ten till noon at my Aunt Marge's, hot dog and bean lunch on the lawn at my cousin Willard's, battle reenactment at three-thirty, and pig-pickin' at six on Nearing River house grounds."

"Sounds like a full day. When does your mother arrive?"

"Her plane comes in at 11:07 in the morning. I have to drive up to the airport to get her, which is about an hour and ten minutes each way. I'll have to miss the genealogy and the hot dogs."

I laughed. "You actually sound sad about it."

He shrugged. "Getting Mom is going to be a little harder than sitting through an ancestor-matching ceremony."

"She sounds pretty awful."

"Oh, no, she isn't. I don't want you thinking that. She's fine. It's just that she doesn't like the family."

"I'm not family," I said, deciding that only one of us at a time could be shy. "Would you like company driving to the airport? I'd rather go with you than hang around putting chili on hot dogs."

Nick beamed at me. "Great. I'd love it." His face closed in again on a frown. "I wonder how I can introduce you."

"How about using my name?"

"Mom isn't very fond of Nearings, except me. She took back her maiden name, you know. She's Mrs. Graham, not Mrs. Nearing."

"I guess she does feel strongly about it."

"Oh well. I'll just say you're a cousin and leave it at that."

That certainly wasn't where *I* wanted to leave it, but he was off the topic of me and onto his mother. It seemed that she was paranoid about losing her luggage. She would bring at least six suitcases to last the six days she was staying and Nick would have to carry them all.

"Six days?" I said. "Mother and I are only planning to buffer through Sunday night."

"Right. It'll be pure unbuffered Mom from then till she leaves."

Actually, his mother sounded pretty neat, although I could see that this problem in dealing with people named Nearing was going to loom rather large. "Do you think she'll be polite?" I said.

"Oh, hideously polite. That's what she does best, being polite. It drives my father crazy."

By that time we were holding hands and I had high hopes for the next ten minutes. "Yoo hoo!" came a voice. "Nancy! Yoo hoo!"

It was my mother, calling for me. Nick and I sighed simultaneously, which was something, although I would rather have done other things simultaneously. We waded back through the relatives to the house. Every single Nearing misinterpreted our hand-holding, and I'm sure none of them suspected that what we were talking about in our low voices was Nick's mother. There were lots of remarks and catcalls, and even one whistle. I said to Nick, "No wonder your mother detests these Nearings."

"They are a little nosy," said Nick.

My mother was almost hopping up and down on the little back porch. "We've found him, honey," she said, and there were tears in her eyes, although she was smiling widely.

"Found him?" I said.

"Your father. We've figured out who he is."

We went inside the kitchen, where a pleasant plump woman was seated at the Sears table, and several people were crowded in there fingering the notebooks spead out in front of her. "This is Elsie Chipley," said Mother. "Her great-grandfather was a Nearing in a little town near here called Scotland Neck. She brought along all her genealogy notebooks and she recognized your father from our wedding picture. She says he's her cousin's son, Robert Nearing."

Elsie did not use the huge rolled charts that Nick's father favored, but kept her facts in three stenography notebooks. The Nearing section of her ancestry seemed to be in the middle portion of book number two. I stared at the little pale green page which had my father's name written on it. "Why did he leave Scotland Neck?" I asked Elsie.

"You know, I wasn't very close to Bob, he was at least fifteen years younger than I. I don't seem to have his birthdate written down here, but as I recall he absolutely detested small town living. He felt cramped and cut off from the day he was born. Yearned for bigger, more exciting things. Other worlds, and other people. I love Scotland Neck, but a surprising number of people feel trapped in the country."

"Do we have any close living relatives?" asked my mother.

"No, not really. Bob's parents died in a car accident when he was in his early teens and he lived with this cousin of mine for a while. They didn't get along too well and Bob definitely didn't want to grow up to work in the family insurance business. And when he didn't marry a local girl, what was there to bring him back?"

"What was his mother's name?" I asked, wondering if my grandmother had been Nelle Catherine, too.

"Mary Elise Spencer," said Elsie. "Now she wasn't from Scotland Neck, she was from farther south. Rocky Mount."

I grinned to myself. Rocky Mount was about thirty miles away.

Nick said, "What's the relationship between Nancy and me?"

"You tell us, Nick," somebody said, and Nick chewed his lip and didn't respond to the quip.

"The relationship to our branch of Nearings," said his father, "seems to be with this common grandfather, here." He tapped a name on his own charts and flipped pages in Elsie's notebooks to show where it came up again. "Samson Nearing, born 1799, died 1881. I'd have to sit down and figure out what you two should call each other, but you're about eight generations removed, counting from Samson down to Nick."

I looked at Nick and my eyes blurred, wondering about that other young man, Bob, son of Mary Elise, who left Scotland Neck for wider worlds.

Elsie Chipley took a pencil from her voluminous purse and very carefully, in a squat but pretty hand, added two names to her little section on Nearings.

Robert Nearing (?)

is what it said. She erased the (?) and wrote in

m. Eleanor Bruce — one dau. — N. C. Nearing

There was something ceremonial about it, there in the kitchen, crowded around a Sears table with a room full of Nearings. My mother looked at the wedding picture of herself and Robert Nearing. I thought it was sad to have to look at a photograph to remember the man you loved enough to marry. The man who died too young to have found many of the wider worlds he wanted.

"Hey, don't cry," whispered Nick in my ear. He pulled me out of the kitchen. I resisted for a moment, thinking maybe Mother needed me, but she caught my eye and smiled a little and nodded. I was glad Mother and I were sharing a bedroom that night. We'd certainly have a lot to talk about.

But I was just as glad to talk about it with Nick first.

Sixteen

That night Nick and I skipped the get-together at the Barbecue House. His father said not to worry; he'd keep an eye on Mother, see she had a good time. Mr. Nearing's interest in us had doubled since he had found the right slot for us on his genealogy tables.

Since hordes of relatives had commandeered all the other cars, we took the "new" station wagon and I drove. "Where are we going?" I said. "Let's not get lost again. Give me very explicit directions. I need to know at least a mile ahead if we're going to turn."

"Actually," said Nick, "I sort of had getting lost in mind. Drive anywhere."

I wondered if I were reading all sorts of unintentional things into that remark. "I'd prefer to get lost someplace picturesque."

"There's a real dearth of pretty spots around here," Nick told me. "Boy, do I understand your father wanting to run out! About all we can go to look at is the sunset."

"Sunsets are the same everywhere, Nick."

"Exactly. So why not watch them from San Francisco or London?"

I turned right on a gravel-surfaced road that looked interesting.

"It isn't," said Nick. "It won't get interesting unless we follow it for five or six hundred miles."

I laughed. "Well, they're not expecting us till midnight."

"Let me drive. Then I won't have to give directions."

"Okay." I stopped the car on the shoulder, put it in park, and slid over to the passenger side. I never drive without a seat belt. It makes me feel unzipped or unbuttoned not to have that strap over me. Nick got in, fixed his belt, and started driving. Now I could see a real drawback to our big wide station wagon. Nick and I were fastened down at least two feet from each other. I should have thought of this, I told myself, and insisted that Mother buy a compact car. Oh, well.

I wondered what Nick was thinking and what he thought of the space between us.

"If I get accepted at William and Mary," said Nick, "I wouldn't be all that far from you."

"No, you could come over weekends if you felt like it."

"That's a nice idea."

He turned left onto a paved road. The sun glared in our eyes.

"Eight generations apart," said Nick. "That's a pretty thin relationship."

I wanted to suggest another possible relationship, but somehow we had gotten awkward again and I lacked the words.

Nick swung onto yet another dirt road and went up a slight hill.

The sun was setting in front of us, beyond the road and the wide fields. The sky was streaked with golden pinks and two jet trails sliced mistily through the colors. It was beautiful.

Nick stopped the car right in the middle of the road and unsnapped his seat belt. He looked at me for a minute. I said, "Are we lost?"

"No."

I unsnapped my seat belt. I had been right about Nick's cheeks. They were raspy.

"The thing is," said Nick between kisses, "you make me nervous."

"Likewise," I said.

"I make you nervous? You always seem perfectly calm to me."

"It's strictly a front. I can tell when you're nervous by your voice. You'd have to take my pulse to tell when I'm nervous."

"What a good idea."

The sun had almost disappeared. The road was apparently never used. Nobody passed us. It got darker and darker. When he paused ("Intermission," said Nick, grinning.) I looked at my watch. "Nick, we've been here for ages."

"Did you have something else you wanted to do?"

But I couldn't think of anything else.

* * *

The following morning we left for the airport at nine-thirty, because, as Nick said, "If I'm not there on time, she'll freak out completely."

Nick's father said, "Drive carefully," in the tone of voice that indicates it wouldn't bother him if you drove carefully in the wrong direction.

"Are you sure your mother won't be upset to have me there, too?" I asked Nick. "Maybe she'd rather have a reunion with you on a one-to-one basis."

"Mom isn't kissy-huggy like all the relatives you've been meeting. That's kind of a Southern phenomenon. She'll look me over and sort of nod approvingly and kind of lean her cheek my direction so I can press my cheek against hers. Then she'll tell me I look quite decent with my hair this way and who is my charming companion? She's very Bostonian."

"I thought she lived in Pennsylvania."

"She does. That's just an adjective Dad used to use for her. She's rather formal and proper and she detests everything Southern. She'll die at the pig-pickin'. Nothing, but nothing, would make her use her fingers to scrape a meal out of a roasted pig."

"I'm not too keen on the idea myself," I admitted.

"Really? Terrific. Mom will approve of you right away. Be sure to tell her you eat only with a fork."

We drove through some heavy traffic then and I didn't talk to him, knowing how I hate it when somebody babbles in my ear while I have to be thinking about tractor-trailers trying to merge into my lane when I'm still in it.

"Actually," said Nick, "I'm sort of worried about your mother."

"*My* mother?"

"Yes."

"Nick, my mother is always a complete and total model of good behavior. What can possibly worry you about her? You're the one who figured her for a buffer, remember."

"Yes, but that was before I realized how much my father likes her. Mom is going to see that right away."

I was struck dumb. I stared at Nick, to see if he thought that was some sort of joke, but he looked perfectly serious. Even worried.

"Dad asked me," said Nick very casually — too casually, "to ask you if your mother has said anything about him to you."

My jaw practically broke my collarbone, falling. "You mean your father likes my mother enough to want inside information about her attitude toward him?"

"You got it." Nick pulled into the airport parking lot and took a parking ticket from the little entry robot. The orange arm lifted and we drove under it. Nick found a space far from the pedestrian exit. "Mom approves of exercise," he explained. "If I park right next to the walkway, she'll think it's because I've gotten slovenly and lazy."

I said, "My head is still reeling about your father liking my mother."

"He's shy. He's afraid to ask her for a date, so he asked her to a reunion instead."

I wanted to ask if this sort of problem ran in the family — asking people to reunions instead of on dates — but I couldn't quite nerve myself up to say it. We sat there. Nick turned off the engine (he'd borrowed a relative's Cadillac so his mother wouldn't have to ride in the jeep or his father's beat-up antique-hauling old van), and with the air conditioning off we were in a beautifully upholstered furnace.

Nick said, "Actually, Nancy, I . . . I . . . kind of identify with how my father feels."

Breathing became hard again, and not just because the car was so hot and stuffy.

"Mother thinks he's very nice," I said. "I know she loved having him come up and work on the antiques with her. They had a good time over that. She . . . she said he was like a teddy bear."

"A teddy bear!" said Nick, insulted.

"You know, huggable. Short and plump and squeezy."

Nick chuckled helplessly. "I don't think that's the description of himself that Dad was looking for. Short, plump, and squeezy. I can kind of see how it applies, though."

"What's *your* mother like?"

"Tall and elegant and untouchable. I think that was one of their problems."

I was stumbling all over those dumb words again. Talking madly away about our mothers and his father when what I wanted to do was talk about *us*. "And you think your mother is going to be bothered by this? After being divorced all these years?"

"My mother is easily bothered."

"Oh, Nick! You look so nervous. I'm sure everything will go all right. I'll be sure and eat neatly and act properly and I'll even chaperone my mother when your father's around. How's that?"

We got out of the car laughing and walked up to the terminal holding hands.

"It's peculiar to think of my father as having a crush on someone," said Nick. "You think of adults as finished with that kind of thing."

"Mother and I talk about how I feel about boys," I admitted, "but she's never said how she feels about men. The subject has never come up. I guess it never occurred to me that she had feelings."

"My father says you can still feel adolescent when you're forty-seven."

We stood on the electric door openers and huge glass walls parted for us. Why couldn't I say, "How interesting! Your father loves my mother and I love you. Now how do *you* feel, Nick?" Instead I had to say, "Look at the board. Her flight's on time. Fifteen minutes to wait."

"Let's go up on the observation deck till it lands."

We dropped our dimes in the turnstile and ran up the stairs to the deck. It was very windy and very hot and there were about twenty other people up there. We sat on the back bench.

"I can't stay with you this afternoon because I have to go straight to Nearing River House to get dressed for the battle," said Nick.

"Don't worry. I'll stick with your mother, maybe, if we hit it off. Your mother and I are only going to the battle to look at you anyway."

Nick picked up my hand, which I had placed in an easily accessible position, and held it. I held his tighter and we ended up in a squeezing contest. "Actually," said Nick, "if I get accepted at William and Mary, you'd be close enough to come stay with me weekends, instead of me going to stay with you. Would you like to do that?"

Words. Honestly. Would I like that? As if I might reply, Nah, forget it, I have better things to do. "Yes," I said, "I'd like that."

We kissed each other and not one of the other observers on the deck observed it, either.

When Nick's mother's plane came in and the passengers began getting off I recognized her right away. The only one who didn't look rumpled from the heat. The one who was, indeed, tall, slim, elegant, and as handsome as Nick. She greeted him just the way he'd said she would. Coolly. Not at all as if it had been eight months since they'd seen each other. I stood back a little, waiting, trying to look like the sort of girl who would only use a fork.

Nick was looking at her with affection and I realized for the first time that one reason he was nervous was that he really wanted her to have a good time. He was just as worried about his mother as he was about his father. That's nice, I thought, I like that.

"And who is your charming companion, Nicholas?" she said, extending her hand to me. She was actually wearing gloves in that ninety-five-degree sunshine. I took her hand and smiled.

"This is Nancy Nearing," said Nick.

"Another Nearing? Another cousin?" Her eyebrows lifted. They weren't cute like Nick's, but very disapproving. I was with her there. I didn't want to be referred to as a cousin either.

Nick shepherded us toward the luggage turntable. He looked at me and I looked at him and we gave each other little half smiles. Nick said, "No, Mom, she's my girlfriend."

My half smile spread quite a lot, and so did Nick's.

"How nice," said his mother warmly, handing Nick her luggage tickets. "Brown leather, dear, with red straps. Three of them. Nancy, I'm delighted to meet Nick's girlfriend. How good of you to come along."

While Nick retrieved the bags we stood to one side and talked about the day's plan and which parts of it both of us planned to go to. My mouth curved in a wide grin I thought might stay there permanently. Because nobody could be happier to hear that Nicholas Nearing had a girlfriend than I was!